"*I need to go to bed.*"

"If that's an invitation, it lacks finesse," he drawled derisively. He was close. Much too close! "But what it lacks in finesse is more than made up for by honesty," he added softly.

"I—you—I didn't mean I needed to go to bed with you!" Surely she hadn't given herself away so completely?

CAROLE MORTIMER says: "I was born in England, the youngest of three children—I have two elder brothers. I started writing in 1978, and have now written more than ninety books for Harlequin Mills & Boon.

"I have four sons: Matthew, Joshua, Timothy and Peter, and a bearded collie dog called Merlyn. I'm in a very happy relationship with Peter Sr.; we're best friends as well as lovers, which is probably the best recipe for a successful relationship. We live on the Isle of Man."

Books by Carole Mortimer

HARLEQUIN PRESENTS
1793—THE ONE AND ONLY
1823—TWO'S COMPANY
1863—ONE-MAN WOMAN

CAROLE MORTIMER

Wildest Dreams

Harlequin Books

TORONTO • NEW YORK • LONDON
AMSTERDAM • PARIS • SYDNEY • HAMBURG
STOCKHOLM • ATHENS • TOKYO • MILAN
MADRID • WARSAW • BUDAPEST • AUCKLAND

ISBN 0-373-11894-5

WILDEST DREAMS

First North American Publication 1997.

CHAPTER ONE

ARABELLA stared at the huge double gates that led up to the house beyond. Forty-eight hours ago she had thought this visit impossible. But as she continued to look down the long driveway she knew that not only was it possible, it was imperative, if she was to salvage any relationship with Merlin at all. Despite what her father and Stephen had done to damage that relationship, she knew she had to do what she could. She still cringed when she recalled the conversation she had overheard between the two men two days ago.

'What do you mean, the man wouldn't even listen to you? You must have—'

'I've told you, Father,' Stephen had cut in exasperatedly. 'I didn't even get in the front gates of the damned house. There were two huge dogs—'

'Stephen! Father!' Arabella had admonished breathlessly as she'd reached the open doorway, entering the room before closing the door behind her. 'I could hear the two of you arguing all the way down the corridor in my own office.' She looked at both of them with questioning blue eyes. 'What on earth is going on?'

Her father's face was flushed, and she guessed that wasn't only due to his undoubted anger; it was three-thirty in the afternoon, and he enjoyed nothing more than a leisurely lunch accompanied by a liberal imbibing of his favourite wine. In fact, it was surprising he was back in his office at all just yet...

As for her brother, Stephen, he certainly wasn't supposed to be here, her father having sent him away on business yesterday, expecting him to be away for several days. Although, from the little she had heard of their heated conversation, it was Stephen's lack of success on his trip that had triggered the argument between father and son.

Her father sat down behind his imposing oak desk, sitting forward to rest his elbows on the green leather top. He was still a handsome man in his mid-fifties, with only a distinguished sprinkling of grey at his temples amongst his dark hair.

His eyes were icy grey now as he looked across the room at his only son. 'Your brother has the answer to that,' he dismissed contemptuously.

Stephen's youthful face flushed resentfully. 'I told you it wasn't my fault, that—'

'"Give him more responsibility," you said,' her father accused impatiently. '"Let him show you what he can do,"' he added scathingly. 'And what happens the first time I try to put that advice into practice?' He slapped his hand down flat on the leather desktop with resounding finality. 'He's sent away with a flea in his ear, that's what happens, just as if he were some door-to-door salesman!' He gave a disgusted shake of his head. 'It's not good enough, Arabella. You and I both know—'

'Let's all just calm down and discuss the problem sensibly,' she cut in soothingly, her suggestion of calming down aimed at the two men; she was her usual unruffled self. She wasn't absolutely sure that the problem under discussion was necessarily her brother's fault; their father had a way of presenting him with impossibilities.

'Stephen?' She prompted him to sit down in the chair facing their father's desk.

An action he chose to rebel against, deciding to sit in the leather armchair at the back of the room, a mutinous expression on his boyishly handsome face; his hair was as dark as their father's, and his eyes were normally a warm blue, like Arabella's own. Normally because, at this moment, Stephen's were stormy with rebellion.

Arabella sighed as she contemplated the two stubborn, arrogant faces, sitting down in the chair opposite her father herself. She loved these two men enormously, but she had to concede that, despite the thirty-year difference in their ages, they very often behaved as childishly as each other. She was often called in as arbitrator between the two, her father impatient with Stephen's impetuous youthfulness, Stephen considering their father old and set in his ways, with a code for business that smacked of the Victorian.

Stephen might have been right in that last accusation, but as owner of a prestigious publishing company that had been in the family for almost a hundred years her father's old-fashioned values made Atherton Publishing what it was. Up here, on the third floor of the building that housed the company, far removed from the rush and bustle of the editorial department of the two lower floors, time seemed to stand still; the furnishings in this office, as in all the executive offices on this floor, looked as if they had come straight out of Victoria's reign.

Which was just the way her father liked it. Arabella too, if she were honest. It was only twenty-five-year-old Stephen who found it all claustrophobic, having left university three years before with a degree under his belt and a lot of new ideas to pull Atherton Publishing into the twentieth century, kicking and screaming if necessary.

Their father's answer to that had been to put Stephen where he could do the least harm: the poor boy had been bogged down for the last three years with the acquisition and distribution of textbooks for schools. It was because Arabella couldn't bear to watch her young brother going quietly insane that she had encouraged her father to give him something more interesting to do. It had taken months of gentle persuasion on her part to get her father to agree, and, from what she had gathered so far from the conversation between the two men, it had not been a successful endeavour.

'Now, exactly what happened?' she prompted her brother soothingly, having great affection for her sibling, although she often felt that her two years' seniority in age was more like twenty! That was probably due to the fact that their mother had died fifteen years ago, leaving Arabella, at only twelve, to become the mother of the family, a role she had taken over all too successfully, if her father and brother's dependence on her were anything to go by.

Stephen's expression lost some of its sulkiness as he looked at her. 'Well, I did as Father asked, and went to see this Merlin chap—'

'Father, no!' She couldn't hide her shocked outrage. The author they all knew only as Merlin was well-known for being one of their most uncooperative, and appeared to be a recluse into the bargain. To have sent Stephen to see him was not only unfair, it was ridiculous. Besides, Merlin was one of her authors... 'Did you send Stephen to talk to him about the film rights to one of his books?' she challenged tensely.

Her father looked a little uncomfortable now, knowing by the glitter in Arabella's deep blue eyes, behind the glasses she habitually wore, that her own temper was beginning to manifest itself. 'You were the one who said Stephen needed to prove himself—'

'But not with Merlin!' She stood up, too agitated to remain seated any longer.

Stephen had been to see Merlin, a man she had been wanting to meet for years, a man who steadfastly refused to agree to such a meeting…!

'Why didn't you tell me where Stephen had gone?' she demanded of her father—although she already knew the answer to that; her father hadn't told her where he had sent Stephen because he had known that if he had, she would have vehemently objected to Stephen going anywhere near 'her' author. All the editors had assigned authors, and Arabella was no exception, although her number was kept to a dozen or so. But Merlin was one of them… 'If anyone was to go and see Merlin, then it should have been me,' she told her father indignantly.

His handsome face creased into a pained expression. 'I'm beginning to agree with you,' he said harshly, shooting another scathing glance at his son.

Arabella knew this wasn't strictly true, that her father was merely hitting out at Stephen again. Because, much as her father valued her, it was as his hostess, the woman who ran his house and social life with such efficiency, rather than as a professional colleague. Oh, she worked at the family company, had an office of her own on this very same floor that was almost as plush as her father's. Nevertheless she had always known her place here was viewed with a certain amount of paternal indulgence, that her father didn't really believe the world of business, especially the cut-throat one that publishing had become in recent years, was the place for a woman—especially a woman as delicate as he preferred to think of Arabella as being.

His view was old-fashioned to say the least, but then, up here in this office, a room that didn't seem to have changed much since her great-grandfather's time, it was easy to see why her father felt that the world of business was strictly for men. Wasn't the fact that her father had sent Stephen to see Merlin proof of that?

She was well aware, no matter what her father was now saying to the contrary, that he didn't believe she should have gone to see Merlin; it had merely been another test for Stephen, one that her brother seemed to have failed. The fact that it had been completely against protocol for Stephen to go to see one of her authors had nothing to do with her father's regret. And she knew it didn't have anything to do with Stephen's either. Her brother, unfortunately, had been brought up in his father's image, and that was primarily to believe a woman's place was in the home, keeping a man's life running smoothly and with as little discomfort as possible.

Arabella had been the one deemed indispensable at home when the time had come for her to go to university nine years ago. The carrot of an office of her own at Atherton Publishing had been merely a sop to keep her living at home. She remembered how pleased she had felt at the time that her father thought her responsible enough for such a position in the company. She should have known better! Within a matter of days it had become obvious to her that the office, and position as assistant editor, was merely an indulgent pat on the head from her father, and that he rarely expected her to be there, usually only during the times when it didn't inconvenience the smooth running of his own life.

No wonder her father had never remarried, she realised now; she had made life altogether too comfortable for him since her mother died for him to need to bother with the permanence of marrying one of the women he had been discreetly involved with over the last fifteen years!

But for the main part she had been aware of what her father was doing and hadn't particularly let it bother her, because in her own quietly stubborn way she had made her mark on Atherton Publishing, and now had several successful authors to her personal credit.

Merlin was one of them, a chance discovery from an unsolicited manuscript submitted five years ago. Merlin—he had refused from the beginning to be known under any other name!—had written a swash-buckling tale of a secret agent working for the English during the Napoleonic wars. Not only was this one of Arabella's favourite periods of history—hence the reason she had been given the manuscript in the first place—but it was also, she'd realised from the very first page, a tale well written: its hero, a Major Palfrey, was a devilishly handsome man who struck a man through with his sword and swept women off their feet into his more than accomplished arms with the same ease, while at the same time allowing neither incident to deter him from his real cause—to aid England.

It was all a *Boys' Own* adventure, Arabella had freely admitted to her father, but, at the same time, the book was so well written it was a pleasure to read; the historical facts, so easily intertwined with the main story, were unquestionably correct.

In fact, Merlin's books were a joy to edit. He had submitted a manuscript a year since that very first one five years ago, all with the same hero, Palfrey. A hero, if Arabella was completely honest, with whom she was half in love...

Robert Palfrey, the gentleman hero of an age long gone, was tall, with over-long blond hair, wicked blue eyes, and a lithe body that he seemed to use to full advantage, whether he was killing the enemy or caressing a beautiful woman. Arabella hadn't been in the least surprised when a Hollywood film company had approached Atherton's several months ago with the idea of putting Robert Palfrey on the big screen. There had been a most successful television series only last year with a similar main character, and the film company had obviously looked around for their own hero to try and cash in on this wave of nostalgia. The Palfrey books were an excellent choice.

Unfortunately, so far, Arabella hadn't been able to convince the author of that. In fact, the two letters she had written to him on the subject had remained unanswered.

Although that was probably an answer in itself. From the acceptance of his first manuscript five years ago, Merlin himself had proved elusive, refusing to come up to London from his home in the south of England to talk with them in person, while at the same time refusing all advances from them to go to his home and speak with him there.

Reclusive hardly began to describe the man, and in five years none of them had ever found out anything about him other than that his name was Merlin; the negotiations over his contract were all done by mail, and always directly with the author himself, the man refusing to employ an agent to act on his behalf. Not that there was ever too much negotiation involved with Merlin; the monies paid were agreeable to both parties.

It was only the use of the single name, Merlin, that had caused some dispute. But the author was adamant, and in the end Arabella had managed to convince her father that this only added to the man's mystique, and therefore to sales of his books. And that could only be good for all of them.

But over the years Arabella had built up a picture in her own mind as to what their author looked like: an irascible old man, with over-long grey hair, a ruggedly tanned face and a wiry body—with a temperament to match the stubbornness he had shown in abundance over the years.

But despite his bad-temperedness Arabella had always thought of him affectionately, a bit like a long-distance grandfather-figure. Having dealt with him personally over the last five years, albeit by mail only—his telephone number was always omitted from his own correspondence—she now deeply resented her father's decision to send Stephen instead of herself to see the man.

'You misunderstood me, Father,' she told him stiltedly as she stood up stiffly. 'By my remark, I meant you had no right sending Stephen to see one of my authors without my permission.' She looked at him challengingly with steady blue eyes behind tortoise-shell glasses; she was a tall woman with a delicate stature, her fiery red hair which she had inherited from her mother secured back in its usual restrictive bun at her nape, her features striking rather than beautiful. At the moment, her small, pointed chin was set at a determined angle.

'Don't go getting on your high horse, Arabella.' Her father sighed impatiently as he saw the angry glitter in her eyes. 'It sounds as if we have enough problems with Stephen being forcibly ejected from this fellow's place, without—'

'Merlin was perfectly within his rights to throw Stephen out,' she said in defence of the author, noting the way her brother winced as he was once again reminded of his humiliating experience. 'Merlin doesn't even know Stephen—'

'He's my son, damn it!' Her father bridled indignantly.

'And who are you to Merlin, either?' she prompted impatiently.

Her father drew himself up to his full height in the high-backed leather chair. 'I own this publishing company!'

She shook her head. 'That wasn't what I meant, and you know it. For the last five years Merlin has been dealing exclusively with *A. Atherton*—'

'For the last five years the man has been a damned nuisance,' her father interrupted irritably. 'He is without doubt the most difficult author we have ever had to deal with, a hermit to the point of being invisible. In fact, I've a good mind to—'

'For the last five years Merlin's books have probably been the mainstay of this company.' Arabella quietly cut in on her father's bluster, sure he was going to come out with a totally nonsensical statement about dropping Merlin from their list.

It was nonsensical even to think along those lines; without Merlin they probably wouldn't have a list at all. Oh, they had other, less successful authors, lots of them, but the Palfrey books had been worldwide bestsellers from the very beginning, and they had remained so.

Even to consider telling an author of that magnitude to find a new publisher simply because he didn't fit in with her father's old-fashioned belief that it was the publisher who mattered and not its writers would be financial suicide at this particular time in the publishing business. Especially with a film contract in the offing. Her father's idea of publishing was about twenty years out of date, and she somehow doubted he would ever catch up.

'There are other authors—'

'Not as good, and you know it,' she said wearily. 'I wish you had told me what the two of you were doing,' she added with a heartfelt sigh. 'I could have predicted the outcome!'

One thing about which Merlin had been consistent in the last five years was his desire for absolute privacy. Stephen's just arriving at his home like that, from Atherton Publishing or otherwise, would not have gone down well at all. In fact, they would be lucky if Merlin didn't tell them he was changing publisher! And that would be disastrous.

She sighed again. 'Someone will have to go down and soothe the poor man's indignant feelings—'

'I'm not going!' Stephen instantly protested, a look

of horror on his face, and appearing so much like their father at that moment. 'The man isn't sane.'

'Well, I'm certainly not getting personally involved in this,' their father dismissed arrogantly. 'I've always thought the man was odd, tolerable only because he's so successful.'

They both turned expectantly to Arabella. Something else she could have predicted. They were so much alike, these two men, with no foresight to speak of; over the years the two of them had come to expect Arabella to be capable of bailing them out of any difficulties they might have dug themselves into. The problem was, she had always managed to do it, too. Although they might just have gone too far this time!

'I'll write him a letter—'

'Do you think that will be enough?' Stephen frowned. 'I—er—I'm afraid I was slightly—vocal, before I left his premises.' He looked uncomfortable now. 'In fact, I may have implied something to the effect of what Father said just now.' He grimaced self-consciously at Arabella's censorious look. 'He was just so damned rude, Arabella,' he said defensively. 'I couldn't let him talk to me that way.'

No, of course he couldn't; he was Stephen Atherton, son of Martin Atherton. God, when would these two learn that the days of champagne parties had passed, that it was the authors that mattered now-adays, for without them there wouldn't be the money to pay for the way her father and Stephen liked to live? It was as well there was one practical member of this family. Although salvaging something out of this mess was going to strain even her efforts at tact and diplomacy!

She shook her head. 'I'll send a letter, but I intend following it up with a visit of my own,' she decided firmly. 'I'll do the first today,' she added decisively, 'before Merlin can come at us with all guns blazing after your cavalier attitude.' With an impatient look at the pair of them, she left the room to return to her own office, intent on writing that letter right away, determined to get it in the post this evening.

Although what she was supposed to say by way of an excuse for her brother's behaviour she wasn't exactly sure. In the end she decided that whatever she said in the letter was sure to be wrong, so she kept it simple, merely informing Merlin that she would be calling on him herself two days hence, unless otherwise notified by him. She knew that the only way Merlin could be sure of reaching her in time to put off the appointment would be to telephone her office, and as the two of them had never so much as spoken on the phone in the last five years she somehow didn't think there was much likelihood of him making that call.

And he didn't. Probably he just intended waiting until she arrived at his home so that he could throw her out too!

But, after the mess her brother and father had made of things, she didn't have too many options left. Besides...she had to admit she was secretly rather curious about Merlin herself. And maybe, just maybe, he would be gentleman enough, like his character Palfrey, not to use brute force on a woman...

She had been intrigued by the character of Palfrey from the first, probably too much so, because over the years he had become the yardstick by which she judged the men who occasionally tried to enter her life. They were invariably found wanting. Oh, she wasn't silly enough to believe the interest of those men was solely in her, anyway; the Atherton publishing company, and the wealth that went along with it, was a natural draw for any ambitious young man, the spinster daughter of the family an obvious catch.

But Arabella had her own ideas about the man she wanted to spend her life with—unfortunately he had lived almost two hundred years ago, and was entirely fictitious, as he existed only between the pages of a book and in the imagination of the man she was hopefully about to meet.

The thought of never again receiving a Merlin manuscript, or losing herself in the life of Robert Palfrey, was enough to harden her resolve to talk to Merlin herself. As far as she was concerned, he could dismiss the idea of a film about his character, as long as he continued to submit those manuscripts about the man with whom she was half in love...

And now here she was, sitting at the bottom of Merlin's driveway, Stephen having given her instructions on how to find the house once she reached the village near which it was situated. In fact, Stephen had been falling over himself to be helpful for the last forty-eight hours, obviously aware he had made a complete hash of his own visit, and anxious to try and make amends.

As she had expected, there had been no telephone call from Merlin in response to her letter, and so she had made her own arrangements to drive down to see him, at the same time hoping she wouldn't have to book into a local hotel for the night; what she really hoped was that she wouldn't be physically ejected from his home, as Stephen had been two days ago.

'Watch out for the two large German shepherd dogs when you get to the gates,' had been Stephen's final warning when she had left the house this morning.

She could see now exactly what he meant by 'large'!

They must be two of the biggest of their breed Arabella had ever seen, with almost identical black and brown coats which seemed to imply some sort of relationship between them. But it wasn't their size, or their loud barks, that kept her firmly enclosed inside her car. It was the fact that they weren't behind the tall gates at all, but leaping up and down outside her car window, the two gates at the entrance of the house having been left open, and so allowing the two dogs their freedom.

Obviously Merlin had been expecting her, she decided ruefully as she watched the two huge beasts slavering on the other side of her car door.

They didn't give any indication of stopping their cacophony of noise. Or of going away. She had a feeling that if she tried to back out onto the road the dogs would follow her, possibly go under the wheels of her car. And, much as she found their behaviour irritating, she didn't want to injure either of them. To drive down the driveway would probably produce the same reaction. Or worse! Which left her with a dilemma: what should she do now?

She had seen a film once in which the leading character had confronted some dogs on their own territory and thereby succeeded in totally disarming them, throwing them into confusion. After all, dogs of this size would be more used to people running away from them than going towards them. It had worked in the film, anyway...!

But this was real life, and both dogs looked to have large teeth and wide jaws, the former, she would imagine, able to do great damage to soft human skin in a matter of seconds. But, by the same token, she couldn't sit here all day just looking at the beasts, and they certainly didn't look as if they were tiring of the game!

Taking a deep breath, she took the bull by the horns—or rather, she challenged the two dogs. She didn't get out of the car slowly or apprehensively but simply thrust open the door, and two seconds later she was standing on the gravelled driveway confronting the animals.

If the situation hadn't been so fraught with tension, the look on their faces might have been laughable; the two huge beasts dropped back several feet in surprise, although their barking continued intermittently. But, as Arabella continued to stare at them, even that died down, and after several minutes they viewed her with what she could only describe as puzzlement. If dogs could look surprised! These two certainly did.

'Where's all the noise gone now, then?' She spoke to them derisively, although inwardly she was mightily relieved still to be in one piece. 'Now, are you going to take me to your master, or do I have to find him myself?'

The dogs continued to look at her quizzically, obviously wondering what she was saying, but seeming to accept, for the moment, that she spoke with a certain amount of authority. Although quite what she should do next she wasn't sure. Would the dogs continue to keep their distance if she made an attempt to walk down the driveway? After all, at the moment she wasn't quite inside the property; maybe the two of them would decide to become protective again if she took a step in the direction of the house?

Well, she could hardly stand here all day hoping someone would come along and rescue her, or that the dogs wouldn't attack. In the circumstances she decided to risk it. The worst they could do was tear her limb from limb.

What a cheery little thought!

She began to walk, the dogs trotting along behind her down the driveway, seeming confused after her audacity in daring to challenge their authority. Which was what she had hoped for.

It was a longer walk than she had thought, though, and as she finally approached the house the two dogs were walking one at either side of her, like escorts, although, to give them their due, they hadn't made any threatening moves.

Arabella could hear the sound of male voices as she neared the house, which became even louder as she turned the last corner.

She came to a gasping halt as she rounded that last bend and saw the house, not impressed by the building itself, but by the two men in the garden outside. Merlin was exactly as she had always imagined him, seated on a low veranda overlooking the garden: a wizened old man well into his sixties, his hair long and grey, skin weathered brown by the many seasons he had seen in his lifetime. Although she had omitted his raggedy beard in her imaginings, a beard as grey and unkempt as his hair.

But it wasn't Merlin who made her gasp, it was the younger man working in the garden below him—a tall man with over-long blond hair, the muscles of his shirtless golden-brown torso rippling as he struggled with the roots of a tree stump that seemed to be proving stubborn. His only clothing, as far as she could see, was a pair of faded denims that rested low down on his hips.

As he became aware of her presence in the driveway he slowly straightened, looking at her with a pair of the deepest blue eyes Arabella had ever seen in her life, and she found herself face to face with the man she was already half in love with. A man straight out of the pages of Merlin's books. Obviously not a complete figment of his imagination, either.

Robert Palfrey was Merlin's gardener!

CHAPTER TWO

'PALFREY' recovered from the unexpected encounter
a lot quicker than Arabella did, his eyes narrowing
questioningly as he looked at her warily. Well, it
wasn't surprising he had got over his amazement
quicker than her; he hadn't just been confronted with
a live, flesh-and-blood hero—more flesh than blood!

Arabella had been instrumental in commissioning
the illustrations for the covers of the Palfrey books—
and if she had met this man beforehand, and given
the illustrator a description of him, she couldn't have
been more accurate. He—

'Who the hell are you?' he suddenly rasped, the
harshness of his voice bringing her out of her dazed
stupor.

Although not enough to actually be able to answer
him, as she was still tongue-tied by all this glistening
male beauty. He *was* beautiful, completely secure in
his own maleness. And so he should be. He—

'Daisy, May—heel!' he instructed the dogs tersely,
and the two animals trotted obediently over to sit at
his feet, salivating for a different reason now as they
gazed up at him, adoringly.

Arabella knew how they felt; she could cheerfully
have sat at his feet and done the same thing herself.
He was real! Robert Palfrey, alive, and standing just
feet away from her.

'I asked you a question,' he rasped again. Those

23

deep blue eyes narrowed flintily as he stood almost protectively in front of the house and its occupants.

'Daisy and May?' Arabella mused, aware that she still wasn't answering his question as to who she was. But she found the names of the dogs so incongruous for two such fierce-looking creatures. They were obviously guard dogs, and yet it was doubtful that calling them Daisy and May would put the fear of God into anybody. Stephen would be mortified when she told him he had run away from Daisy and May!

'Palfrey's' mouth tightened at her slightly mocking tone. 'Don't be fooled by the names,' he bit out sharply. 'They guard what they're meant to guard!'

Merlin! Arabella realised, her mind suddenly returning to exactly why she was here. Coming face to face with this man had just thrown her totally.

'I'm sure they do,' she dismissed smoothly. 'I'm actually here because I have a business appointment with Mr—er—Merlin,' she amended awkwardly, peering around 'Palfrey' to where the elderly man still sat on the veranda.

Those deep blue eyes narrowed even more. 'You do?' He sounded sceptical.

Didn't she look the part? She had checked her appearance very carefully before she'd left the house this morning to drive down here. Admittedly, the jacket of her dark grey pinstriped suit was still in the car at the end of the driveway, but, even so, the smart white blouse and straight skirt that reached just above her knees, the neutral-coloured tights and moderately heeled black shoes were surely quite businesslike? Her hair was in its usual bun at her nape, her glasses rested firmly on the bridge of her nose; in what way didn't she look the part?

'I do,' she assured the younger man briskly, recovering a little now from the shock of actually meeting the real, live Palfrey; after all, she wasn't here to see this man at all, but the elderly one seated behind him. Having got this far without actually being thrown out, she intended to make the most of her opportunity. Especially since she had been so angry with her father and Stephen two days ago; it would be too humiliating if she ended up being treated the same way. 'I wrote to him and told him of my arrival this afternoon,' she added pointedly, wishing he would get out of the way so that she might speak to Merlin himself.

The younger man scowled frowningly. 'You did?'

Much as she had initially been bowled over by this man's devastatingly good looks, she was now starting to find this conversation with him irksome. After all, it was Merlin she had come here to talk to, not his gardener! 'If I could just have a few private words with Merlin.' She tried to look around the younger man to where his elderly employer sat listening to them unconcernedly.

'Concerning what?' the young man prompted tersely.

There was something very odd going on here. Merlin hadn't spoken a word since her arrival, and the blond man was distinctly hostile; surely the gardener was overstepping his duties by speaking for his employer in this way? Unless he also acted as security guard to the older man? But even so...! 'My name is Atherton—'

'It's the publisher, boyo.' The elderly man spoke for the first time, his voice gravelly, as if he didn't use it very often. He stood up, moving to stand beside the younger man, the two of them looking slightly ridiculous together, one so tall and golden, the other shrivelled with age. 'Is that right, miss?'

'Quite correct.' She nodded in confirmation, at last feeling as if she was making some sort of progress. 'I wrote to you—'

'You're A. Atherton?' Again it was the younger man who spoke to her.

Irritation flickered in her eyes as she gave him a brief glance. 'Arabella Atherton, yes,' she dismissed impatiently, looking at Merlin with some surprise as he began to chuckle throatily. The chuckle soon became a fully fledged cackle.

What was so funny about her name? Admittedly it sounded as if it came from another century, but her mother had loved to read historical novels, her father often saying he thought his wife would rather have been born in earlier times. But, even though Arabella had found her name a bit of an encumbrance when she was younger, she now found it rather attractive. It was certainly different.

'I realise the two of us have never been formally introduced.' She held out her hand, taking a couple of steps closer to Merlin, careful of the dogs as they began to growl low in their throats. 'But we have been writing to each other for the last five years.' She smiled warmly. 'I'm Arabella Atherton. And you're—'

'Andrew, the gardener.' The chuckling had stopped, although the elderly man still grinned his amusement. 'The aged family retainer,' he added pointedly.

'Your age only comes into it when it comes to up-rooting stubborn tree stumps,' the younger man said dryly. 'The rest of the time you take pleasure in telling me how fit you are!'

'But I am, boy.' Andrew grinned at him before turning back to Arabella. 'He's Merlin.' He nodded in the direction of the man Arabella had come to regard as Palfrey.

This young man, his muscular body still glistening and golden after the exertion from his efforts with the tree stump, a man who might have posed for the Palfrey book covers himself, was actually the author of those books? Merlin was Palfrey? No, Palfrey was Merlin! The two were one and the same person?

The elderly gardener chuckled again as Arabella and Merlin stared at each other. 'I think you may have come as much of a surprise to her as she has to you, boy,' he murmured wryly.

Merlin's mouth tightened, his gaze flinty as it swept scathingly over her businesslike appearance. 'I had assumed A. Atherton was a man,' he finally acknowledged contemptuously.

He wasn't pleased to discover his editor was actually a woman, Arabella realised, her cheeks becoming flushed.

'I think the two of you made some erroneous assumptions concerning each other.' The elderly gardener still sounded amused by the situation.

Merlin shot him a look of irritation. 'Go and ask Stella to put the kettle on, and we'll all have a cup of tea.'

'Certainly, sir.' Andrew pulled on an imaginary forelock. 'Right away, sir.' He nodded before turning to walk around the side of the house, disappearing into what Arabella assumed must be the kitchen.

Merlin's irritation had deepened to a scowl. 'I think

I've allowed him too much familiarity over the years,'
he muttered with a shake of his head.

Familiarity breeding contempt? Somehow she
didn't think so. The two men obviously liked and respected each other very much; an easy affection existed between the two.

'A cup of tea would be very welcome, thank you,'
she said, smoothly changing the subject. And it wasn't
a lie either; she had been driving for several hours
and a cup of tea certainly wouldn't come amiss.

He frowned across at her and then reached down
to the ground to pick up a pale blue denim shirt, pulling it on over the wide width of his shoulders before
buttoning it up the front.

Arabella's breath left her in a gentle sigh. She
hadn't even been aware she was actually holding it
until that moment, able to breathe a little easier now
that Merlin was more formally attired. Although she
was still stunned at his physical likeness to his character. She was always advising would-be authors to
write about what they knew, but it was the first time
she had actually found that the author and the hero of
his books were one and the same person!

'I told your husband the other day that we have
nothing to talk about,' he bit out coldly.

It took Arabella a couple of seconds to realise exactly whom he was referring to. 'Stephen is my
brother,' she corrected him, smiling at the thought of
someone like Stephen being her husband; there were
only two years' difference in their ages, but to her
Stephen had always been a child. He had done nothing since joining the company to make her think any
differently of him.

Merlin regarded her thoughtfully, head tilted to one

side. 'There's no family resemblance,' he finally murmured ruefully.

She knew that, had always been aware of the fact that Stephen had inherited their father's undoubted good looks, whereas she—well, she wasn't sure who she resembled! She wasn't like her tiny, beautiful mother. She wasn't exactly plain, but she certainly wasn't a beauty either. She seemed to fall short, somewhere in the middle of the two, not ugly, but having nothing remarkable about her features.

More than one man in the past had assumed that, as in the movies, if her hair were loosened and her glasses removed she would suddenly be transformed into a beauty. Those men had been bitterly disappointed! Her red hair was indeed a beautiful colour, but released about her shoulders it took on a will of its own, becoming completely unmanageable. And without her glasses her eyes ceased to be big, blue and intelligent, surrounded by dark lashes, and simply became myopic; it was obvious at a glance that she was as blind as a bat. So much for the transformation!

'I can assure you, he is my brother,' she replied without rancour. After all, she was what she was. 'I can only apologise for the way he just turned up here unannounced a couple of days ago,' she added with a frown. 'I wasn't aware he had done so until he arrived back at the office.'

'Spitting fire at my rough handling of him, no doubt,' Merlin guessed—accurately!—a wry twist to his lips.

Arabella smiled in return. 'To put it mildly,' she acknowledged.

The dark blue eyes narrowed. 'And now you've

been sent to calm the troubled waters,' he derided mockingly.

'I haven't been "sent" anywhere.' She gave a firm shake of her head. 'I'm hoping that the only troubled waters we have are those back at the office; I left my father and brother in no doubt as to how I felt about their interference in our relationship,' she explained grimly, having assured her father before she left this morning that if she couldn't straighten this situation out he was going to hear more on the subject.

'"Our relationship"?' Merlin echoed softly.

She could feel the heat in her cheeks at the obvious mockery in his tone. 'That of author and editor,' she clarified sharply. 'I—'

'Tea's ready, boy,' Andrew called from the house.

'Perhaps Miss Atherton has decided not to stop for tea,' Merlin returned dryly, although his gaze remained firmly fixed on Arabella.

'Of course she wants tea, boy,' the gardener admonished tauntingly. 'Do you think she's driven all the way down here to be sent away without even a cup of tea?'

Arabella knew that her father would agree with Merlin's earlier remarks about Andrew's familiarity; the servants at their family home were rarely seen, never heard, and the household ran like clockwork. But it was obvious that these two were more than employer/employee, that they had a friendship that seemed to go back years. Merlin should consider himself blessed, not cursed, she thought.

'Tea would be lovely,' she accepted lightly; at least she was going to get inside the house! 'Although perhaps I should go and get my bag and lock the car up before I do that,' she added thoughtfully.

This might not be London, but she still didn't want to leave her bag in an unlocked car some distance from the house. When she'd arrived earlier she had thought it best not to have anything in her hands that might look in the least threatening. But she had some paperwork in the car that she would need if she were to talk to Merlin.

'Will the dogs be OK now?' She still hesitated about making any sudden moves in their presence.

Merlin eyed her with a scowl. 'You took a risk earlier, just getting out of your car like that.'

It had either been that or turn tail and run, as her brother had done. After her contemptuous anger towards the two male members of her family, she'd had no intention of doing that. Although she had a feeling that might have been the reason Merlin had left them loose in the first place...!

'I won't be a minute,' she assured him lightly.

'No hurry,' he dismissed with a careless wave of his hand. 'Just make your way back to the house when you're ready.' He turned towards the house, the two dogs trailing obediently at his heels.

Arabella gave a rueful smile to herself as she walked back to her car. Although things had certainly changed since her father had first taken over Atherton Publishing twenty years ago, a time when the publisher had wielded the power, most of their authors were nevertheless still thrilled at a visit from their editor. Merlin had made it obvious her being here was just an inconvenience to him. But then, he was one of the best-selling authors of today and would immediately be snapped up by another publishing company if he were to find they were invading his privacy.

After collecting her bag, she made her way into the

house by the same way the gardener and Merlin had, finding herself walking straight into the kitchen. The two men were seated at a solid oak table that dominated the centre of the spacious room, while a lady in her sixties provided them with tea, cakes and scones. The latter looked mouth-wateringly home-made, but after her long drive Arabella had to admit it was the tea she was most interested in.

'My wife, Stella.' Andrew introduced her as Arabella came hesitantly into the room. 'This is Rob's publisher, Stella,' he explained with relish, obviously still greatly amused that his employer's editor had turned out to be a woman.

Arabella had hoped to discover what Merlin's first name was; after all, not everyone could call him 'boy'. Especially as he must be in his late thirties. Rob? She looked at him sharply. Could it be that his name was Robert, like his hero? He didn't seem about to tell her!

'Please call me Stella,' the housekeeper invited warmly as she placed a steaming cup of tea on the table in front of Arabella, having seated her beside Merlin.

'Arabella,' she returned lightly, before gratefully sipping at the tea.

'What a pretty name,' the housekeeper said spontaneously. 'Sounds like one of your heroines, Rob.' She smiled at her employer; she was a small, plump woman, with hair almost as white as her husband's, and brown eyes that twinkled as much too. Obviously this was a happy household, even if their employer was more than a little taciturn.

Merlin grunted at the comment, his gaze fixed morosely on the bottom of his teacup as he drank from it. Physically, Arabella acknowledged, he looked just like his hero, Palfrey, although there were no laughter-lines on this man's face, no warmth or humour in his blue eyes, something the Palfrey character had in abundance. But Merlin wrote the Palfrey books, so he must be possessed of a sense of humour. Mustn't he...? Not when it came to unwanted visits from his editor, obviously!

Suddenly he stood up abruptly. 'Shall we take our tea and go through to my study?' He looked at her with coldly compelling eyes.

'Of course,' Arabella agreed; at least he was going to talk to her. It was a step further than Stephen had got, and that had to be better than nothing. She directed an apologetic smile at the elderly couple as Merlin instantly turned on his heel and walked out of the room, leaving Arabella with no choice but to follow him. She wasn't apologising for Merlin's behaviour—the couple must be used to that by now—she was apologising for not doing justice to the afternoon tea the housekeeper had provided; Merlin hadn't given her time!

His study was like that of so many other authors she had seen: the desk was the dominating feature, a large leather-topped mahogany one in this case, behind it a bookcase full of reference books. The only difference she could see in this room was the lack of a word processor; most authors used them nowadays. But Merlin's manuscripts were always neatly presented, so he had to have one somewhere, making her wonder if this was actually the room that he used to work in.

'Sit down,' he invited curtly, already seated across

the desk from her himself, the dogs on either side of him.

Now Arabella knew what it felt like to be a prospective published author seated across from her in her own office: a bit like being back at school and being hauled before the headmaster for some misdemeanour. And the dogs definitely added to the feeling of menace in the room. As the seconds, and then minutes, passed once she had sat down, that feeling didn't diminish!

'I take it you did receive my letter?' Arabella was finally the one to speak.

'Yes,' he confirmed harshly, leaning back in his high-backed leather chair to look at her with narrowed eyes.

'So my being here isn't unexpected?' she persisted determinedly; remembering the dogs and the open gates, she knew damn well it wasn't!

'A. Atherton's presence here isn't unexpected,' he acknowledged coldly. 'Your presence...' He gave a dismissive shrug. 'I had no idea the A stood for Arabella.'

Or he would have asked for another editor years ago, the accusing statement implied. Did the fact she was a woman mean she wasn't a good editor?

'I had no idea your first name was Robert, either,' she said lightly, but just as pointedly.

He was silent again for several long seconds, and then his mouth twisted wryly. *'Touché.'* He nodded in acknowledgement of the challenge in her voice.

It was strange, really, but here, in the privacy of his study, Robert Merlin had taken on an even more familiar appearance. Of course he reminded her of his hero, Palfrey, but there was something else too, a definite feeling that she had seen him before some-where. But where? And surely she would have re-membered it if she had? With his golden good looks, and powerfully attractive face, he was a man who would be very difficult to forget. Yet she knew she had seen him before somewhere, knew—

She straightened in her chair as she realised she was staring at him, and that he was returning that stare with questioning eyes. 'Sorry.' She blushed ruefully. 'It's just—you aren't quite what I was expecting either.' That had to be the understatement of the year! 'But then we've agreed the feeling is mutual,' she added briskly as she sensed a sarcastic reply was about to leave his lips. She put down her empty tea-cup. 'I have some papers in my bag for you to look at—'

'If it's about the filming of Palfrey, then I'm not interested,' he interrupted harshly.

Arabella looked up from picking up her bag. 'You can't possibly know that until you've seen what the film company has to offer,' she pointed out gently, not wanting to antagonise him further but at the same time aware of just how lucrative the film contract could be for him. For Atherton Publishing, too, she acknowledged ruefully, sure that he would lose no time in pointing that out.

It was obvious, from this house and the presence of the elderly couple who worked for him, that he was comfortably off. And she knew better than most how much money he earned from the Palfrey books. But the film company was talking major money for this author. It would be slightly reckless on his part, she felt, to say no to the idea without even looking at the contract...

His mouth twisted derisively. 'Palfrey would become a Hollywood caricature—with all the hype that goes along with it!' he dismissed easily.

Arabella took out the offending contract before snapping shut her bag. 'I'm sure the film company will be completely open to negotiation about your own amount of involvement in things.' After his obvious reluctance to talk to them at all, they seemed agreeable to any terms he cared to make! 'With a contract to match,' she added encouragingly.

'A contract they would instantly break, if and when it suited them to do so,' he returned scornfully.

'Of course they wouldn't!' she gasped indignantly.

'Just how many Hollywood contracts have you, or your publishing company, been involved in, Miss Atherton?' he said tauntingly.

Atherton Publishing was not that sort of publishing company; had made its name and money mainly from educational books. It had been Arabella who had introduced successful contemporary fiction to the list, and Merlin was definitely her most successful author to date. A fact which, looking at the intelligence in those blue eyes, she had a feeling Robert Merlin was completely conversant with!

'How many have you?' she returned somewhat tartly, knowing she was getting nowhere with this man.

The mockery left his face as his expression hardened once again, a tense stillness settling over his muscular frame. 'I don't have—'

'Daddy, I'm in the swimming team!' The study door had burst open, and the excited statement had come from the young lady who stood framed in the open doorway.

Despite her considerable height, she was young, Arabella realised, probably about thirteen or fourteen, poised on the brink of womanhood. Raven-black hair fell silkily past her shoulders, her glowingly lovely face had none of that puppy-fat that could be so annoying at her age, and her body was tall and slender, with the promise of curves yet to come. In another couple of years she was going to be a stunningly beautiful woman.

And she had called Merlin 'Daddy'...

Arabella looked at him with new eyes. There was a Mrs Merlin somewhere, then...?

It was ridiculous of her to feel surprised, even faintly disappointed. Robert Merlin must be the most attractive man she had ever seen in her life; of course there would be a woman in his life, possibly even a wife. The latter was not just a possibility; the existence of his daughter was proof of that.

'Daddy, did you hear what I said?'

'Of course I heard you, Emma,' he acknowledged indulgently. 'But can't you see we have a guest?' He gave a pointed look in Arabella's direction.

Eyes the same deep blue as her father's suddenly became shy as the young girl looked at Arabella. 'Sorry,' she murmured ruefully. 'I didn't mean to interrupt you, but I couldn't wait to tell Daddy my good news,' she added determinedly.

Arabella smiled her sympathy, remembering occasions when she had rushed home to tell her own father equally exciting news from school. Unfortunately, it had only been exciting to her, her father listening with a complete lack of interest. Although Robert Merlin didn't look uninterested; it was just that she happened to be taking up his time at the moment.

She smiled at the young girl. 'I'm sure your news takes precedence over anything I have to talk to your father about,' she assured her lightly.

'What are you and Daddy talking about?' Emma asked guilelessly, moving to perch her bottom on the side of her father's desk.

'Emma!' her father reproved abruptly.

Arabella couldn't help laughing softly at the young girl's unrepentant expression. 'I'm from your father's publishing company, and—'

'A. Atherton?' The deep blue eyes glowed interestedly.

Robert Merlin sat up straighter in his chair behind his desk. 'And exactly what do you know about A. Atherton?' he said slowly.

Emma grinned at Arabella, completely unabashed by her father's grim expression. 'Are you A. Atherton?' she persisted. 'I always had a feeling you might be a woman.'

'And just why the hell did you feel that?' her father demanded impatiently.

She shrugged slender shoulders. 'Just the tone of the letters.'

'And what sort of tone might that have been?' Robert Merlin frowned at his daughter in complete bafflement.

The young girl grinned unconcernedly. 'Unfailingly polite and reasoning—even when you were at your rudest!' She gave her father a mischievously teasing look. 'I always thought another man would have given you back as good as you gave.'

Her father looked outraged. 'I was never rude!'

Emma Merlin gave Arabella a conspiratorial grimace. 'Oh, I think you'll find that you were, Daddy.

Although I'm sure Miss Atherton forgave you,' she added soothingly as he still looked furious at the accusation.

Arabella was impressed with the maturity of this young girl. And her perception! Her own father and Stephen had often been incensed by this man's fanatical wish for privacy—as witnessed by the blundering way Stephen had tried to force his way in here two days ago! Arabella had always respected that wish for privacy, often diverting the attention of the media away from this popular author.

It was a view her father and Stephen didn't share. In their opinion, if Merlin wanted the glory—and the money!—his writing brought, then he also had to accept some of the negative aspects, and that included interest in his private life. To her father it wasn't a negative aspect anyway...

Yes, Emma was right; if Merlin's editor had been either her father or Stephen, then he would have been handled very differently.

'Of course,' Arabella confirmed smoothly.

Robert Merlin looked far from pleased at the slightly patronising air the two females seemed to have adopted towards him, his blue eyes flinty and cold. 'I was not—'

'Your father is such a wonderful writing talent,' Arabella continued conversationally to Emma. 'He could be forgiven most things.'

'Except killing off Palfrey,' Emma returned disgustedly. 'That has to be the silliest thing—'

'Emma!' her father exploded. 'Will you kindly shut up?' He glared at her fiercely.

Arabella looked from father to daughter, Emma appearing stubbornly determined in the face of her father's anger. But it was to Robert Merlin that Arabella turned her full attention. She couldn't have heard Emma properly.

He couldn't possibly be thinking of killing off Palfrey!

CHAPTER THREE

'WELL, Miss Atherton?' Robert Merlin looked at her challengingly across the width of his desk. 'Do you have something to say on the subject, too?'

Something to say? If it was true, she certainly did have something to say!

'You can't be serious!' was all she could manage at the moment. He couldn't—could he...?

His blue eyes remained flinty as his gaze raked across the shock that was so evident on her face. 'I thought I was the ''wonderful writing talent'', Miss Atherton?' he finally drawled.

'Y-you are.' She spluttered the confirmation of her earlier statement. 'But—'

'Is there a ''but'', Miss Atherton?' he cut in with quiet intensity.

The way he kept so pointedly calling her 'Miss Atherton' was beginning to grate on her already frayed nerves. Of course there was a 'but'; the Palfrey series of books were the most popular to appear on the market for some time—and Robert Merlin appeared to be about to kill off his hero!

'Emma.' The author turned to his daughter with raised brows as she watched the exchange with obvious enjoyment. 'Don't you have some homework you should be getting on with?'

'I—'

'Or something?' he added determinedly, making it obvious he felt she had said enough for one day.

'Not really,' she replied, unabashed, obviously completely secure in her relationship with her father.

'Then I suggest you go and find something,' he told her bluntly, obviously just as secure in his relationship with her!

Emma stood up with a fluidity that would become graceful elegance as she got older. 'OK,' she accepted good-naturedly. 'I'll see you at dinner,' she told Arabella lightly, frowning as she saw the regretful look on her face. 'Daddy!' She looked at him incredulously. 'You *have* invited Miss Atherton to dinner?' She sounded shocked at the possibility that he might not have done so.

And Robert Merlin looked far from pleased at that censorious look. 'I—'

'You can't possibly expect Miss Atherton to drive all the way back to London without even feeding her,' the young girl admonished him. 'After all, she came all this way just to see you.'

Arabella could see that not only did Robert Merlin not expect to have to feed her, but that he had no intention of doing so!

Again she had to admit that his response at meeting his editor wasn't the usual one; most of her authors were only too pleased to have personal interest shown in them. But then, Robert Merlin wasn't like any other author she dealt with!

He gave an impatient sigh. 'I hadn't been talking to Miss Atherton long enough—before your interruption!—to have the chance to make a dinner invitation,' he snapped pointedly.

Emma again looked completely undaunted by her father's abrupt behaviour. 'Well, make one now, and

then tell Stella we have one extra for dinner.' S
gave him a cheeky grin.

Two sets of deep blue eyes warred for several long
seconds before Robert Merlin broke the battle of wills
with another irritated sigh, and turned impatiently towards Arabella. 'You'll stay to dinner?' he said
harshly.

It was far from the most gracious invitation she had
ever received, and if she had any sense she would turn
it down. But on a professional level she knew she
couldn't do that, knew she had to at least try to persuade Robert Merlin that he was committing professional suicide by killing off his main character,
Palfrey. She doubted very much that he could create
another series that the public would take so much to
their hearts. Or she to her own!

'Thank you,' she accepted, just as stiltedly.

He turned to his daughter. 'Satisfied?' he rasped
irritably.

'Of course.' Emma grinned, moving to kiss him
lightly on the cheek. 'I'll see you both later, then,'
she added with satisfaction.

Arabella was still too stunned by the news that
Merlin was considering killing off Palfrey to respond
to Emma's conspiratorial wink as she left the study.

'I apologise for my daughter,' Robert Merlin murmured distantly. 'She can be over-familiar at times.'

'Unlike her father,' Arabella replied without thinking, colour darkening her cheeks as Robert Merlin
raised dark blond brows. 'I'm only stating the obvious, Mr Merlin,' she added awkwardly, although she
had a feeling it was too late to worry about offending
this man; he was so prickly, it was impossible not to
offend him.

'Unlike her father,' he conceded dryly, looking at her with renewed interest, as if—unlike everyone else in this household!—he had just realised she was a woman.

Arabella felt her cheeks grow hot under that intense scrutiny, suddenly aware again of her own appearance—of how businesslike her clothes were, of her hair secured at the nape of her neck, and the glasses perched on the end of her nose. She wished she were blonde and stunningly attractive, and had the sort of body men looked at. But she wasn't, and she didn't have, and perhaps that was why she was still unmarried at twenty-seven...!

'I'm sorry.' She broke his gaze awkwardly. 'That was extremely rude of me.'

'Yes, it was,' he acknowledged slowly. 'But it was also honest.'

She shrugged. 'I'm always honest, Mr Merlin—'

'Robert,' he put in mockingly. 'The formality is ridiculous in the circumstances.'

She couldn't have agreed more. But she had had the impression that formality was what he preferred. 'And, as you know, I'm Arabella,' she invited stiltedly.

He relaxed back in his chair. 'As Stella remarked earlier, it's a fitting name for one of Palfrey's ladies.'

In view of the fact that in her mind he had become Palfrey, was the living image of him, that was a very unnerving thing for him to say. 'If what Emma was saying earlier is correct, then there aren't going to be any more Palfrey ladies.' She turned the subject away from the disturbing thought of herself as Robert Merlin's 'lady'; the man, by the mere evidence of Emma's existence, was married, for goodness' sake.

He visibly bristled. 'As well as being over-familiar, my daughter is also indiscreet!'

'But also truthful?' Arabella prompted guardedly; after all, he hadn't actually confirmed yet that he intended killing off Palfrey.

'Yes,' he rasped.

The baldness of the statement was enough to tell her he really meant it; he was going to kill Palfrey! She couldn't believe it; she felt as if she had just been told that someone she loved was about to die.

'They must be traits she inherited from her mother,' Arabella murmured distractedly.

'Let's leave Emma's mother out of this!' Robert Merlin was no longer relaxed in his chair; his whole body was rigid with tension as he sat forward, his mouth set in a grim line.

That she had touched on a sensitive subject was obvious. Perhaps there was no Mrs Merlin after all; divorce, unfortunately, was all too common nowadays, and Robert Merlin wouldn't be the first man to have claimed custody of the children from a marriage. But that Emma's mother had been beautiful could be in no doubt either. Emma's colouring and looks were nothing like her father's; only her height, perhaps, could be attributed to him, and of course the blue eyes.

But if Merlin found the subject of his wife a painful one Arabella had no interest in pursuing it either!

'Certainly,' she dismissed gladly. 'I would much rather discuss Palfrey anyway.'

His mouth twisted impatiently. 'I'm sure you would, Arabella, but, as I'm sure you must realise only too well, I don't discuss my work with anyone.'

Being his editor for the last five years had certainly

not involved too much work on her part; Robert Merlin had just periodically submitted manuscripts to her, never asking her for advice or guidance on the storylines as some authors did, and rarely did any actual editing need doing either: the manuscripts were always perfectly presented and written.

'Except Emma, apparently,' she pointed out lightly, still deep in thought as to how she could actually get this man to listen to reason over such drastic action where his hero was concerned. Arabella, for one, would be very upset if Palfrey were to die, and that wasn't just from a professional point of view.

'Not even with Emma.' He shook his head. 'She happens to have taken a computer course at school during the last year,' he explained at Arabella's puzzled frown, 'and now insists on putting all my work on disk. I write in longhand, Arabella,' he elaborated dryly. 'I had someone come in to type up my manuscripts for me before Emma decided she could do it on her computer.'

That explained the lack of a wordprocessor or typewriter in this room. She had had no idea that Merlin wrote his manuscripts out by hand, still really knew nothing about him. Except that he was going to kill off Palfrey!

She frowned. 'What are your reasons for killing off Palfrey?'

He shrugged dismissively. 'It's time.'

Time for what? How could she, and millions of other readers, not have the publishing of the Palfrey books to look forward to? 'I don't agree.' She shook her head decisively. 'In what way is it time?'

'He's outlived himself.' Robert Merlin's tone was implacable. 'It's time to move on to something else.'

Incredible. Palfrey wasn't just a character in a book for her, he was real, and she was sure that millions of other people felt the same way.

But she was, after all, Merlin's editor. 'Do you have another series of books in mind?' She kept her tone businesslike.

'Possibly,' he returned noncommittally.

Arabella bit back her increasing frustration at his lack of cooperation. 'It's going to be very difficult to follow a series as popular as Palfrey's—'

'I like a challenge,' he dismissed easily.

'It's a move Palfrey fans may not like,' she told him evenly. 'May not like'! If they felt anything like she did, they would be devastated at the news!

'Then the sooner I finish this book and get started on the new series the better,' he said unconcernedly.

She wasn't getting through to him at all. Or maybe she was and he just didn't care... He had already lived in this large house with its extensive grounds when he had first sent her a manuscript, so the assumption had to be that he had been relatively wealthy even before he'd begun writing, which meant he wasn't doing it for the money. Which meant she couldn't cite loss of earnings as part of her argument for not disposing of Palfrey.

'Robert.' Was it her imagination or did her voice deepen huskily at her use of his first name...? 'You don't seem to understand—'

'Oh, I think I do,' he assured her dryly. 'And I also think,' he added briskly, 'that my daughter may have a point about your drive down here.' He frowned. 'I'll have Stella show you to a guest bedroom with adjoining bathroom; that way you can freshen up and have a rest before dinner.'

In other words, the conversation was over. But at least he wasn't throwing her straight out as he had Stephen. Although she was sure that was due to Emma, and not to any belated show of manners on Robert Merlin's part.

She didn't kid herself that the extra time here would give her a chance to talk to him again about the Palfrey books; Robert Merlin's expression was implacable.

'That would be nice,' she accepted politely.

She needed time to think, anyway, to try and work out exactly what her next move should be. If there was one!

His mouth twisted, as if he knew exactly what she was thinking—and was amused by it. 'I'll call Stella.' He nodded, standing up to cross the room and open the study door.

Arabella winced as his voice boomed out the name of his housekeeper. Her father would have paled at such indelicacy; their own home, under Arabella's guidance, ran smoothly and efficiently, with the minimum of fuss. But it had been obvious, by their familiarity, that the couple who ran this house for Merlin were friends as much as anything else, perhaps necessarily so for a man trying to bring up a young daughter on his own.

She again felt curious about Mrs Merlin, although she was already sure that Merlin himself would never enlighten her. She hadn't even known he had a daughter until a short time ago.

Stella grinned good-naturedly at her employer as she joined him in the doorway, obviously used to his method of summoning her.

'Miss Atherton is staying to dinner, Stella,' Merlin

informed her abruptly. 'Show her to a bedroom she can use for the moment, and give her directions for the dining-room for later. We'll eat at eight o'clock,' he added dismissively as he moved to sit behind his desk once again.

If the housekeeper was surprised she was staying for dinner then she didn't show it, chatting lightly as she showed Arabella upstairs to what had to be a guest bedroom: its cream and lemon decor was attractive but impersonal.

'This is lovely.' Arabella turned to thank the older woman.

'I'm cooking lamb for dinner,' Stella told her. 'I hope you like it; it's Rob's favourite.'

Arabella had a feeling that, for all its informality, this household was run pretty much as 'Rob' liked it. 'Lovely,' she accepted with a bright smile. 'It's my favourite too!'

The housekeeper looked pleased. Arabella waited until the other woman had left before dropping down wearily on the bed. She had come here prepared to persuade Robert Merlin to listen to the film company's offer concerning the Palfrey books—and instead it looked as if there might be an abrupt end to the series!

'Hi.' Emma grinned as she stood outside the bedroom door. 'I thought I'd come and take you down to dinner.'

She looked so innocently beguiling that Arabella didn't have the heart to tell her Stella had given her perfectly adequate instructions earlier for finding the dining-room.

'Come in,' she invited the young girl. 'I was just

in the middle of fixing my hair.' She gave a rueful grimace as she indicated her loose tresses.

Emma moved gracefully into the bedroom, having changed out of her school uniform into a pair of black leggings and a loose white shirt. 'Pretty wild, isn't it?' she conceded as Arabella secured it in its usual knot at her nape. 'Have you ever thought of having it cut?' She tilted her head consideringly to one side as she sat on the bed watching Arabella. 'It's such a lovely colour; I'm sure it would look great cut short.'

Arabella had never thought of cutting her hair; she had always worn it long. 'The ugly duckling doesn't really turn into a swan,' she teased lightly.

Colour darkened the young girl's cheeks. 'I wasn't for a moment suggesting— You aren't an ugly duckling!' she protested awkwardly.

Arabella felt sorry for her; she hadn't meant to embarrass her. 'Forget it, Emma,' she dismissed easily.

'But I really meant it,' the young girl insisted. 'I've always wanted red hair,' she added wistfully.

'But you have beautiful hair,' Arabella chided.

'You see.' Emma grimaced. 'I guess we all want what someone else has. Did you have any luck with Dad earlier?'

'Luck?' Arabella blinked, a little taken aback at the sudden change of subject. What did Emma mean? Surely her infatuation with the way Robert Merlin looked hadn't been so obvious that even his daughter had noticed it? How embarrassing!

'In persuading him not to kill off poor old Palfrey,' Emma explained lightly.

Phew! That would teach her not to jump to conclusions. Just because she was all too aware of how devastatingly attractive she found Robert Merlin, that was no reason to think everyone else knew it too. She had almost given herself away just now! Palfrey was a much safer subject than his author...

'He refuses to discuss it.' Arabella shook her head.

'But I bet you don't want to talk about anything else,' Emma returned knowingly.

Arabella was starting to wonder if Emma's appearance at her bedroom door was quite as innocently helpful as it had first appeared; the young girl obviously wanted to talk to her alone on the subject of the Palfrey books. But Arabella knew Robert Merlin well enough now to know that he wouldn't welcome her discussing his personal business with anyone, even his daughter.

'I think, for the moment, that I have to bow to your father's wishes,' she said guardedly.

'But—'

'We're going to be late for dinner if we don't go downstairs now,' Arabella continued in a friendly tone. 'And I have a feeling your father is a stickler for punctuality,' she added teasingly.

Emma stood up. 'He's a stickler for most things,' the young girl conceded with a grimace. 'But you can't possibly let him kill off Palfrey—'

'Emma,' she reproved her firmly, brows raised over blue eyes.

'But—'

'Let's go and eat.' Arabella opened the bedroom door in preparation for leaving the room. 'I don't know about you, but I'm starving.'

Emma's mouth was set in a determined line as she accompanied Arabella down the stairs. Obviously she wasn't pleased at having her plan to speak to Arabella alone about her father's writing actually foiled by Arabella herself!

Arabella felt quite sorry for the young girl and regretted putting this barrier between them. She would have liked to have at least one ally in this household but, by the same token, she couldn't run the risk of alienating Robert Merlin any further. If that were possible!

Emma cheered up the moment she saw her father was already waiting for them as they entered the dining-room, crossing the room to kiss him warmly on the cheek. 'You're looking very handsome this evening.' She looked at him speculatively, at his dark grey suit and snowy white shirt, the former making his hair look more golden than ever as it brushed over his collar. 'To what do we owe the pleasure of seeing you so smartly dressed for dinner?' she added teasingly. 'I'm sure it isn't for my benefit!'

In all honesty, his appearance had taken Arabella's breath away the moment she'd entered the room. If anything, he looked even more attractive in formal clothing than he had in his jeans earlier! So Arabella was glad, for the moment, to have the respite of father and daughter talking. If only to gather her scattered wits!

Robert Merlin looked far from pleased at having his daughter draw attention to the fact that he obviously didn't usually dress for dinner. 'We have a guest, Emma,' he reminded her harshly, before turning to Arabella. 'Would you like a drink before dinner? Perhaps a glass of wine?'

She just hoped her voice came out normally! 'Wine. Thank you,' she added huskily. God, this was awful; she was here on business, not to act like a gauche schoolgirl—as if she were no older than Emma—just because she had come face to face with the man she had been fantasising about for years!

And she *had* been fantasising about him, she realised shakily; Palfrey, with his daring escapades and winning way with the ladies, was the reason why no other man she had met in the last five years had measured up to her dreams. And Robert Merlin was rapidly becoming Palfrey in her mind...

If she hadn't believed in love at first sight, she did now.

She was in love with Robert Merlin!

CHAPTER FOUR

IN LOVE?

Of course she wasn't in love with Robert Merlin. She didn't even know the man!

In lust, then?

God, yes! Every time Arabella so much as looked at him she felt a quiver of awareness run down the length of her spine. In lust... What an admission from someone who had only ever known lukewarm passion with the few men she had dated over the years—even with Malcolm, the man she was seeing now. This feeling of physical awareness was like nothing she had ever experienced in her life before. And—

'More wine?'

Arabella suddenly became aware that Robert was talking to her. As she blinked up at him dazedly, she couldn't for the life of her have said what it was he had been talking to her about. Something to do with wine, she thought. But she already had a full glass—

'Your glass is empty,' he prompted, frowning at her preoccupied stare. 'I wondered if I could get you some more wine.'

Her glass was empty! When had she drunk the contents? She didn't remember taking so much as a sip. Yet she had drained the glass dry.

'Yes, please,' she accepted awkwardly, thrusting her glass forward.

She watched him from beneath lowered lashes as

he turned to get the wine bottle. Unlike the rest of her family, she didn't usually drink alcohol, and had only accepted one glass out of politeness. But the white wine had disappeared unnoticed. Almost. Because she did feel a certain warm glow inside...

Although that could be due to the close proximity of Robert Merlin. He was *very* close as he refilled her glass, so close she could smell the aftershave he wore, see the damp tendrils of hair at his nape: he must have showered before changing to come down to dinner—

Her imagination instantly took her one step further as she allowed her thoughts to conjure up a picture of what he must have looked like as he'd stepped into the shower—

Stop!

She simply had to stop thinking about him like this, otherwise she was going to be a quivering wreck, incapable of speech. Incapable of anything!

She took another desperate gulp of wine, becoming accustomed to it now—in fact, it was starting to taste quite pleasant!

'I'd go easy with that if I were you,' Robert drawled.

She blinked up at him, once again amazed at how tall he was. Although she was sure that the difference in their heights wouldn't be too apparent if they were both horizontal—

She was doing it again! Good grief, she was never going to be horizontal with this man! How her brother Stephen would laugh if he knew about half the erotic thoughts that had been going through her head since she'd first seen Robert Merlin; a 'professional virgin' was how her brother saw her. Well, she didn't feel very virginal at the moment!

'It must be some time since you ate lunch,' Robert explained. 'I would hate to be accused of getting you drunk,' he added dryly.

Lunch? She hadn't bothered to stop and eat lunch on her way here. But that was nothing unusual; she very often didn't eat the midday meal, found it tended to make her sleepy. But this evening she was just aware that breakfast had been her last meal, ten hours ago!

'I've never been drunk,' she assured him brightly, very much aware as she did so that her voice, usually of low modulation, sounded much too loud. Or maybe it was just that her hearing had become extra-sensitive...?

He shrugged unconcernedly. 'There's a first time for everything,' he murmured, before turning to re-place the cooled white wine in the ice-bucket.

There certainly was—and minutes ago she had been contemplating her first time in bed with a man. This man!

Ludicrous! The idea of that actually happening was so ridiculous, it was laughable. There might not be a visible Mrs Merlin, but there surely had to be a woman in the life of a man as sexily attractive as Robert Merlin.

The glowing euphoria caused by the wine wore off, bringing a sudden jolt back into reality. She was a twenty-seven-year-old spinster, with unmanageable hair, glasses, and the sort of figure models had craved in the Sixties: shapeless and very thin!

There was absolutely nothing there to attract a man of Robert Merlin's calibre, a man certainly handsome enough to play the part of his own character in the film he refused to allow. A character he intended killing off in his next book, apparently...

Her fall back into reality was complete with this realisation: Palfrey was to die.

'You're being rude again, Daddy,' Emma admonished him. 'I'm sure Arabella is old enough to know whether or not she wants more wine!'

Robert Merlin looked at Arabella consideringly, seeming to take in everything about her in that one sweeping glance. 'More than old enough, I would say,' he finally murmured in agreement.

She wasn't that old, for goodness' sake. He made her sound like Methuselah! Did she really look so much like an old maid?

Probably better not to press for an answer to that question; as Stephen would say, she probably wouldn't like it!

How depressing. Maybe she should go to the hairdressers and have something done with her hair, and contact lenses were always a possibility; she had just never found the time in her busy schedule so far to wrestle with the initial period of wearing them. There was nothing she could do about her figure, though; she would never develop the voluptuous curves men seemed to find so alluring; she simply didn't have that sort of shape and never would. But she could change the way she dressed—

Stop! she told herself again.

It was ridiculous to let her mind run off at a tangent like this after one meeting with the man of her dreams. Even with all those changes, she would still be Robert Merlin's unwanted editor, intruding into his private life. And after today she was sure he would make certain that it never happened again.

She was grateful when, at that moment, Stella arrived with their first course: beautifully arranged prawns with avocado. Arabella was also relieved to see that the large round table was big enough for her not to have to sit too close to Robert Merlin, although it was still conducive to conversation.

Conversation which Arabella left mainly to father and daughter as she took the opportunity to collect her thoughts. She had struggled for years to be taken seriously as a businesswoman, but, in the last few minutes, she had been acting like any other gauche female. It simply wouldn't do!

She was here for a purpose, one of even more importance than she had at first realised, after what Emma had disclosed earlier.

'—driving back to London this evening?'

She looked up as she caught the tail-end of Robert Merlin's question and realised it was addressed to her. 'I had initially intended to, yes,' she answered him steadily. 'But now I think it would be better if I stayed at a local hotel. Perhaps you could recommend one?' she prompted lightly, knowing she wasn't going to be up to that long drive back to London once dinner had finished.

Besides, she still hadn't managed to talk to Robert about the subjects that needed to be discussed. Probably because he didn't feel they had to be discussed at all!

'I—'

'We can't possibly let Arabella go to a hotel, Daddy,' Emma put in protestingly, frowning at her father. 'We have plenty of room here. Arabella could use the bedroom she was shown to earlier.' She stated the obvious.

Arabella should have realised the young girl might make such an offer. In normal circumstances she would have been only too pleased to accept. But these weren't normal circumstances. Besides, she noted that the offer hadn't been seconded by Robert Merlin!

'Actually, Emma—' she turned to the young girl '—I would rather go to a hotel.' She smiled to take any offensiveness out of the statement; the truth was, the further away from Robert Merlin she was in the immediate future the better.

'Why?' He was the one to rasp bluntly.

Why? She certainly couldn't tell him the reason why! Having a twenty-seven-year-old virgin infatuated with him wasn't something he would welcome, she was sure.

'I've imposed on your hospitality long enough,' she told him lightly.

He returned her gaze mockingly. 'You aren't imposing at all, Arabella,' he finally told her smoothly.

Too smoothly! They both knew that, given the choice, Robert Merlin would not even have her sitting at his dining-table. So why was he being so pleasant now about her being here? To put her in an awkward position, came the answer without hesitation. It would serve him right if she accepted Emma's invitation!

But she knew that she wouldn't, because that would mean spending more time in Robert Merlin's company. The sooner they returned to the impersonality of corresponding by mail the better; that was the way Arabella would like it. Although she doubted she would ever forget that she had met the real, live Palfrey.

'Nevertheless—' she shook her head in refusal '—I

think it would be better if I did go to a hotel.' She met the challenge in his gaze.

'But that's silly.' Emma was the one to answer now. 'Besides, it's going to be quite late by the time we finish dinner,' she added pointedly as Stella began to clear away their empty plates in preparation for their main course. 'Daddy, tell Arabella she can't possibly go to a hotel at this time of night,' she instructed firmly.

'Andrew said to tell you he's brought Miss Atherton's car up to the house,' Stella put in lightly, before leaving the room with the used crockery.

Arabella turned to Robert Merlin with raised brows; she'd had no idea her car had been moved.

'You left the keys inside,' Robert drawled dismissively. 'Besides,' he added hardly, 'you had parked it so that it was impossible to close the security gates.'

Ah, this was probably more like it; her car had been in the way, so it had had to be moved.

'That settles it, then,' Emma said with satisfaction. 'Daddy has locked up for the night,' she explained, at Arabella's puzzled look.

Arabella didn't consider it settled at all; Robert Merlin could simply unlock those security gates and she could be on her way. 'I didn't bring any overnight things with me, Emma.' She continued to refuse the invitation gently, determinedly not looking at Robert Merlin, although she sensed his mocking gaze was still on her.

'That's no problem at all,' Emma instantly dismissed. 'You can borrow something of mine.'

'But—'

'You've already agreed that you won't be able to

drive back to London this evening,' Emma pointed out happily.

'Well, yes. But—'

'Then you must stay here,' Emma declared. 'Mustn't she, Daddy?' She turned to him to support her in her determined invitation.

He continued to look at Arabella with those mockingly hooded eyes. 'My daughter can be very stubborn when she sets her mind to it.' His amusement at her obvious discomfort was there in his drawled tone. 'She seems to have set her mind on having you stay here tonight!'

Arabella was glad he found this all so damned funny! 'That must be a trait she inherited from you!' she returned sharply; after all, he was absolutely fanatical about maintaining his privacy.

Also, she noted, he still hadn't actually seconded Emma's invitation...

'Possibly.' His mouth tightened ominously now, eyes narrowed to icy slits, as his amusement disappeared. 'I suggest we eat Stella's perfectly cooked food, and return to this subject later,' he added harshly as the housekeeper returned with a tray laden with hot dishes.

There was nothing to return to as far as Arabella was concerned; she was going to stay at a hotel!

What a turnabout from when she had set out this morning. All she had been interested in then was getting to see Robert Merlin at any price—now she couldn't wait to get away from him! But this morning she could have had no idea of the devastating effect this man would have on her, couldn't possibly have known—

'—you should telephone?'

She blinked across at Robert Merlin as she realised he was talking to her once again—and she was lost in her own thoughts once again. If this carried on he was going to think she was a complete moron!

'Sorry?' She frowned.

He gave what could only be described as an impatient sigh. 'I said, and I should have thought of this earlier, is there anyone you should telephone? To let them know you're safe and well, and that you won't be returning this evening?' he added as Arabella continued to look at him blankly.

There was her father and Stephen, she supposed. Although when she had left home this morning it had been with the angry avowal that she wouldn't be returning until she had managed to speak to Robert Merlin and put things right between them; when she didn't return tonight they would just assume she was having the same difficulty as Stephen in achieving that! They would probably even be amused at the thought.

'No, I don't think so, thank you,' she refused politely. Even Malcolm, the man she was seeing at the moment, wouldn't be overly concerned at her absence; they met two or three evenings a week, neither of them questioning the other as to their activities on the other four or five nights.

Arabella had a feeling Malcolm saw someone else then. But he was pleasant enough company on an occasional basis, and so she considered that what he did with the rest of his time wasn't really her business. After all, she didn't want to marry the man, just go out with him sometimes. It wasn't exactly a passionate affair, but then she had never been overwhelmed by physical desire for any of the men she'd been out with.

She had never been overwhelmed by physical desire at all, until now!

Until she'd met Robert Merlin she hadn't even known what physical desire was. She wasn't absolutely certain she wanted to know, either; Robert Merlin was as unattainable as the stars to her.

'No eager young man waiting in London to hear from you?' he returned mockingly now.

Malcolm was in his late forties, so he didn't fit the description of being either eager or young. 'No,' she answered abruptly. 'This lamb looks delicious.' She determinedly changed the subject, having no intention of discussing her private life—or lack of it!—with this man.

Robert continued to look at her with mockingly raised brows for several seconds, easily holding her gaze, and a frisson of awareness seemed to spark between them across the table. It felt so intense to Arabella, so fraught with tension, that she glanced over at Emma to see if the young girl could feel it too. But Emma was happily helping herself to a selection of vegetables, seemingly unaware of any atmosphere.

Her blue eyes returned almost shyly to Robert Merlin, only to find he was scowling now, his own eyes dark with displeasure. But, even so, Arabella couldn't break that gaze again, feeling a little like a butterfly caught on a pin. This man was playing with her, exerting his will over her without saying a word. And it had to stop!

She determinedly broke the intensity of that demanding gaze. The effort of doing so caused her hand to shake as she took the vegetable dish from Emma. But she studiously avoided looking at Robert Merlin again as she helped herself to the vegetables she liked.

Arabella was glad of Emma's presence at the table over the next hour or so; both she and Robert talked to the young girl while, at the same time, managing not to address a single word to each other. Well, that suited Arabella perfectly; she didn't know what to say to Robert Merlin any more anyway. Her own nerve-shattering response to him was paramount.

By the time they were served with coffee, it was a little before ten o'clock. Emma refused the strong brew—that, too, was probably just the way Robert liked it!—in favour of going to bed, explaining she had school in the morning. Arabella instantly pan-icked at the thought of being left alone with Robert Merlin and decided it was time she made an exit too.

'I'll get something for you to wear tonight,' Emma told her before Arabella could say anything about leaving.

In fact, Arabella had already opened her mouth to make her own excuses, only to close it again with a noticeable snap at Emma's remark.

Robert chuckled, the first time Arabella had heard him do so—and it had to be at her expense! A shiver of delight ran down the length of her spine at the husky sound. 'Give in to the inevitable, Arabella,' he drawled, amusement still sparkling in his deep blue eyes. 'As we've already agreed, Emma can be as stub-born as me when she sets her mind to it.'

Arabella certainly knew how stubbornly determined he could be! 'Very well.' She decided it was probably better to accept this gracefully; two Merlins ganging up on her was two too many! 'But if you don't mind

I would like to go up to bed now too.' The good food and wine were starting to make her feel sleepy. Besides, it had been a long, traumatic day.

'And if I do mind?' Robert challenged softly.

'Daddy!' Emma protested at his rudeness.

He shrugged unconcernedly. 'Maybe I have some business I need to discuss with Arabella.'

'In that case...' Arabella had stood up to leave the table, but she sat down again now. After all, talking to Merlin was what she was here for.

'You are a bully, Daddy,' Emma told him affectionately. 'Don't tease Arabella any more tonight; she looks tired.'

Teasing? Was his behaviour this evening Robert Merlin's idea of teasing? If it was, Arabella didn't appreciate it!

Neither did she appreciate the tense silence that descended over the room with Emma's departure. The air seemed to crackle with electricity as Arabella waited—and waited!—for Robert Merlin's business discussion to begin.

Finally Arabella could stand the tension no longer. 'What business do you want to discuss with me?' she prompted tensely.

He returned her gaze calmly. 'I don't,' he dismissed with a shrug.

Her eyes widened. 'But—'

'I only told Emma that *maybe* I had some business to discuss with you,' he pointed out mockingly. 'The truth of the matter is, we've already discussed anything that needed discussing.'

Arabella didn't agree with him; her earlier conversation with him had been quite unsatisfactory. But she was too tired to argue with him on that point just now.

What she really needed was to get away from here—from Robert Merlin's devastating likeness to his character, Palfrey!—and do some serious thinking about what to do about this situation. She certainly couldn't think straight in the company of Robert Merlin!

But she couldn't calmly leave here knowing he intended to kill off Palfrey, either.

The truth of the matter was, her attraction to Robert Merlin meant she was too close to the situation, that she couldn't deal with any of this with her usual tactful, businesslike efficiency. How could she be any of those things when every time she looked at Robert she just wanted to launch herself into his arms, to feel the melting pressure of his lips on hers, to know the force of his hard body moulded to hers, to—?

She stood up again. 'I need to go to bed,' she told him abruptly.

'If that's an invitation it lacks finesse,' he drawled derisively, also standing up, instantly towering over Arabella. And he was close. Much too close! 'But what it lacks in finesse is more than made up for by honesty,' he added softly, his warm breath stirring the tendrils of hair on her temple.

'I—you—I didn't mean I needed to go to bed with you!' she spluttered in confusion—and embarrassment. Surely she hadn't given herself away so completely? Robert's last remark seemed to imply that she had!

Had she? Did this man know just how much being near him affected her? Surely she hadn't been so inept at hiding her inner turmoil since first meeting him? Because if she had—

He chuckled softly at her obvious confusion. 'How old are you, Arabella?' he mused ruefully, one slender hand moving up to smooth back those loose tendrils at her temple gently.

His touch reduced her to jelly; her legs felt weak, her heart seemed to thunder loudly in her chest. Surely he couldn't hear that too? No, she was sure it was just the blood rushing through her veins.

How old was she? Arabella inwardly grasped at the question—but for the moment she simply couldn't remember her age! And 'old enough' certainly wasn't the right reply to make in the circumstances! How old was she? She felt like that pinned butterfly again, held immovable by eyes that were a deep, unfathomable blue.

'It doesn't matter,' he dismissed gruffly. 'I was merely engaging in the game of verbal flirtation just now, Arabella—teasing you, as Emma would put it.' His voice had hardened slightly. 'Not preparing to leap on my reluctant guest the minute we are alone!'

'I'm not reluctant—I mean—' Dark colour heated her cheeks as she realised she was just making this situation worse. If that were possible. The thing was, she had never really indulged in what Robert called 'the game of verbal flirtation'.

Her father and brother believed her to be cool, calm, and capable, but at the moment she was none of those things. She was so hot she felt on fire, and she was shaking so much she could hardly stand. As for being capable, she couldn't have moved from this spot if her life had depended on it. Although she was very much afraid her reputation as Merlin's editor did!

That marauding hand cupped one of her cheeks now, his thumb lightly caressing her lips. 'You're an intriguing combination, Arabella.' He spoke softly, al-

most to himself. 'Obviously very experienced in your
career, very good at what you do, and yet as a woman
I could swear—'

He broke off, frowning darkly, a look of anger
tightening his mouth. 'But looks can be deceptive,'
he added gratingly. 'I've never met a woman who
wasn't other than how she appeared—and I don't intend getting involved with one ever again!'

Arabella was so stunned by this harshly made accusation that she didn't even have a chance to avoid
the mouth that descended so rapidly onto hers, claim-
ing her lips with a savagery that took her breath away.

Robert's arms were like steel bands about her waist,
moulding her body against the hardness of his, making her aware of every sinewy contour. Not that
Arabella needed to be made aware of him—her whole
body was tingling with a desire that made her feel
dizzy, aware of nothing else but this man and the way
his mouth moved so sensually against hers.

His hair was soft and silky to her fingertips. As she
clung to him her fingers became entangled in that
over-long silkiness and the kiss deepened, Robert's
tongue moving enticingly against her lips, his—

Suddenly she was no longer in his arms; her fingers
were no longer entangled in the hair at his nape. Now
Robert was standing several feet away from her, his
expression grim, only the heavy rise and fall of his
chest telling of his own disturbed senses.

Arabella blinked dazedly. 'I—'

'What can we do for you, Emma?' Robert's attention wasn't on Arabella but on his daughter as she
stood in the doorway.

How long had Emma been standing there? was
Arabella's first horrified thought. Had she seen them

in each other's arms? It was obvious that her father wasn't at all happy at the prospect that she had.

Emma was eyeing both of them curiously; if she had seen the two of them together moments ago then she wasn't about to let them know that!

But the conversation between father and daughter would give Arabella the necessary time to pull herself together; if either of them addressed a remark to her now, she didn't think she would be capable of answering. Not with any degree of sense, anyway.

What had happened just now? One moment Robert had been full of anger—at her? She wasn't even sure of that—and the next she had been in his arms with his hungrily demanding mouth on hers. Oh, he had been quietly goading her all evening, engaging in that game of 'verbal flirtation' as he called it, but she had had no idea it would result in her being swept into his arms and kissed until she felt dizzy with longing!

'I brought some night attire down for Arabella,' Emma answered her father now, at the same time holding up the blue garment she had in her hand. 'As I said I would,' she added defensively as her father continued to glare at her.

'You could have left it in the bedroom for Arabella,' Robert rasped harshly.

'I—'

'Which is where I suggest you take it now,' he added coldly.

'But—'

'Now, Emma,' her father bit out forcefully, a nerve pulsing in his cheek.

'But I—'

'Just do it, Emma,' he ground out between clenched teeth, as if he was exerting a great force of will so as not to totally lose his temper. Which he probably was! 'You've interrupted a private conversation between Arabella and myself,' he added with icy challenge.

Emma might have been accustomed to her father's rudeness, to the fact that he was very often impatient, with her as well as with other people, but she certainly didn't appear to be at all familiar with his anger being directed at her. Though it wasn't now, not really. It was misplaced anger; Robert was angry with someone else entirely. Whether with himself or with her Arabella wasn't really sure, but poor Emma was the one bearing the brunt of it.

Tears filled Emma's eyes, tears she seemed determined not to let fall as she blinked them rapidly away. 'So I gather,' she returned tautly before turning on her heel and hurrying away.

'Emma!' Robert instantly called after her—a call she chose to ignore as she ran up the stairs without even a glance back at her now anxious father.

'I'll go to her.' Arabella lightly touched his arm.

Robert looked at her but didn't actually seem to see her, lost in his misery at having dealt so harshly with his daughter, because of an anger she wasn't even responsible for.

Arabella still didn't really know who he was angry at, didn't know who was responsible for what had happened between them just now, and she still had no idea how she had ended up in his arms, being kissed by him so passionately—

But she didn't want to think about that just now, couldn't think about it, or she would end up a quivering wreck again.

'I'll go up and speak to her,' she told Robert.

'I told you,' he muttered from behind her. 'Trouble.

Getting involved with any woman causes nothing but trouble!'

Arabella quickly left the room, not looking at him before she did so. Because she couldn't.

In all honesty, she had no idea what she was going to say to Emma. But she would think of something. She had to. She would be leaving here tomorrow, and what had happened between herself and Robert Merlin certainly wasn't important enough—to Robert, anyway—to leave a lingering friction between father and daughter. She would find something appropriate to say!

She caught up with Emma just as she reached her bedroom, following the young girl into the room.

After which she couldn't have spoken if she had tried!

Emma sat down dejectedly on the side of her bed and, as she did so, Arabella couldn't help her attention being drawn to the large, framed colour photograph that stood on the bedside table. It was of a woman, a woman laughing lovingly in the direction of the photographer, and her likeness to Emma was all too apparent. Although it wasn't this likeness that had all of Arabella's wide-eyed attention.

Emma looked up at her silence, followed the direction of her gaze and picked up the photograph, running a loving finger over one peachy cheek. 'My mother,' she told Arabella proudly. 'But she lives in America, so I don't see her very often,' she added wistfully.

Arabella had thought Emma strikingly attractive when she'd first met her, but whereas Emma was still blossoming into womanhood this lady was breathtakingly beautiful, stunningly so, her face dominated by huge violet-blue eyes, her features perfectly sculptured. In fact, she was a vision of perfection.

She was also someone Arabella instantly recognised!

Emma's mother's identity answered so many questions for Arabella. Now she knew exactly why Robert Merlin guarded his privacy so determinedly, and the reason for the dogs and the security gates!

She also knew the reason why he had looked so familiar—Palfrey aside—when she'd first seen him earlier. It must be seven—no, probably six years since she had last seen him. His hair was longer now, and the years had added a hard maturity to his face, but she knew him nonetheless.

CHAPTER FIVE

'GOOD grief, Arabella! Your hair! What have you done to it?'

Arabella looked up from the manuscript she had been reading, sitting at the desk in her office, to smile ruefully at her brother. 'What do you think I've done to it?' she returned mockingly.

Stephen came fully into the room, crossing the carpeted floor to sit on the side of her desk. His head tilted quizzically to one side as he looked down at her critically. 'Well, it's an improvement, I must say.' He finally nodded his approval.

Arabella gave another smile. 'From you, that's quite a compliment.'

And, in truth, it was. Although she didn't really care what Stephen, or her father, had to say about the fact that, after wearing her hair long all her life, she had been to the hairdressers and had it styled so short it was almost boyish. Almost. Because the stylist had left wispy tendrils that brushed against her cheeks and the nape of her neck; the red of her hair was now a deep burnished copper.

Arabella had been amazed at the transformation the new style had made; her eyes appeared huge and haunting, those wispy curls against her cheek emphasised the perfect sweep of high cheekbones and a smooth jawline. Until last night she hadn't even realised she had cheekbones!

Even to her own eyes she had looked almost beau-

tiful when she'd gazed at the reflection that stared
back at her in the mirror, once the stylist had blow-
dried those soft curls. The difference it made was incredible. All the wild disorder of her hair was gone,
and in its place there were soft, copper-coloured curls.
She was inwardly very pleased at the change, felt a
new confidence in herself.

Stephen smiled back at her speculatively. 'So who
is he, sis?' he prompted conspiratorially.

She returned his gaze coolly. 'Who is who?'

Her brother grinned down at her. 'Oh, come on,
Arabella, don't act dumb. You know very well what
I mean. In the last week you've stopped wearing your
glasses in favour of contact lenses, and those severe
business suits you always wore to work have been
replaced with more feminine—feminine but expen-
sively tailored—clothes,' he amended as he saw she
was about to protest at his description of the fitted
black trousers and grey silk blouse she wore.

Stephen couldn't possibly know this, but underneath those trousers and blouse was black lacy underwear of a kind she had never purchased before. It
was amazing really, but she had never realised how
silk underwear, unseen by anyone but herself, could
make her feel so completely feminine, no matter what
her outer clothing might be.

A week, Stephen had just said. Was it really only
a week since she had left the Merlin house so
abruptly? Somehow it seemed much longer...

She had managed to mumble something conciliatory to Emma that night, before stumbling back to the
bedroom she had been assigned. She had forgotten to
take the nightgown with her when she'd left Emma's
room, but that really hadn't mattered, because she

hadn't got into bed but had lain sleepless on top of the covers. That photograph next to Emma's bed, the woman who was so easily identifiable, that beautiful, beautiful woman, had been Robert Merlin's wife...

Her head had buzzed with her discovery. Robert Merlin's wife had been beautiful, incomparable. God, who would ever have guessed that *she* had been Robert Merlin's wife? It was incredible, absolutely incredible, and made Arabella's own feelings where he was concerned all the more ridiculous. Whatever had prompted him to kiss her, it certainly hadn't been because he was attracted to her. How could he be, when he had been married to someone so breathtakingly lovely, someone he had loved so very much?

In the circumstances she couldn't exactly blame him for his bitter feelings towards women. He had been hurt very badly by Emma's mother, had shut himself away here in England to lick his wounds after the divorce.

And she'd known there was no point in her even trying to discuss the making of a Palfrey film in Hollywood; Robert would never allow it. She was wasting her time. And his.

Somewhere near dawn Arabella had fallen into a deep sleep, exhausted by her tortuous thoughts. When she'd woken up again it had been shortly after nine o'clock in the morning, and her movements had been hurried and disjointed as she'd prepared to leave.

She had found only Stella in the kitchen, the other woman informing her that Robert was driving Emma to school, but that he should be back shortly. Arabella had never felt so relieved about anything in her life before, hurriedly explaining to Stella that she had to

leave now, that she must get back to London immediately.

To the poor woman's puzzlement, Arabella had refused to stop long enough even to have a cup of coffee, hurriedly writing Robert Merlin a thank-you note,
assuring him that Atherton Publishing would be in
touch with him in the near future.

Daisy and May had been sitting out in the driveway
near her car, but they'd given her only a cursory
glance, seeming to accept that their master had allowed her to arrive, so they could let her leave. If
only they'd known; their master didn't feel strongly
enough about her one way or the other to care whether
she stayed or left!

So Arabella had gone. So fast, she might have been
pursued by demons.

In a way she had been. Yes, she wore glasses. Yes,
her hair was unmanageable the way it was. Yes, she
was too thin. And yes, there was no way Robert
Merlin would ever see her as anything other than an
unwanted nuisance invading his privacy.

Yes, all of those things were true, and the last she
could do nothing about. But the others she could!

In the following week, as Stephen had so accurately
noted, she had. She still wasn't ravishingly beautiful,
never would be, but, as her brother had also noticed,
the changes were certainly an improvement.

'There has to be a man involved in all this,'
Stephen persisted now. 'Surely you haven't fallen for
dear old Malcolm after all?' he added mockingly, having made his contempt for the older man obvious from
the first time they had been introduced.

Arabella raised dark auburn brows. '"After all"?'

'Well, goodness knows the man has been hanging

around long enough,' Stephen dismissed easily. 'But I thought it was nothing serious between you two?' He frowned at the thought that it might be otherwise. 'He isn't the man for you, Arabella,' he added with a shake of his head.

'I'm well aware of that and, no, it's not serious,' she confirmed easily.

Malcolm had seemed totally bewildered by her new appearance in the last week. Whereas the few romantic feelings she had had towards him had disappeared completely after meeting Robert Merlin, the changes in her had sparked Malcolm's interest—so much so that, whatever his other interests had been, he seemed to have dropped them now, pushing her to see him most evenings, invitations that, for the main part, she had managed to refuse politely with the excuse of other commitments.

She could never hope to match the beauty of Robert's wife, but, by the same token, Malcolm could never be Robert Merlin either! Despite what she now knew about Robert's wife, he was still entangled with Palfrey in her mind; her attraction to the author was stronger, not weaker, for having met the man himself.

Stephen shrugged. 'Well, as I've already stated, there has to be a man involved in this somewhere!'

Arabella sat back in her chair, looking up at her brother derisively. 'What a typically chauvinistic remark.' She shook her head disgustedly.

Stephen grinned unabashedly. 'Of course. I'm the first to admit what a chauvinistic pig I am.'

She smiled at him affectionately. 'You should know better than most that Father isn't a particularly good role model to follow, Stephen,' she drawled mockingly. 'You—' She broke off as the telephone began to ring on her desk, giving her brother an apologetic smile as she answered the call. 'Yes, Di?' She acknowledged their telephonist and receptionist.

'There's a man asking to speak to you, Arabella.' Di sounded a little breathless.

'Who is it, Di?' Her attention was still half on her brother.

'He refuses to give his name, Arabella.' Di sounded apologetic. 'But he says he wants to talk to you.'

She sighed. 'Unless he agrees to give his name, don't put him through.' Would-be authors often telephoned in this way once they had sent in a manuscript, not seeming to realise that it could be weeks before an unsolicited manuscript was dealt with. They were usually gently, but firmly, told they would have to wait until they were contacted by mail, rather than being put through to someone like Arabella. In fact, she was surprised Di hadn't done that in the first place.

'You don't understand, Arabella.' Di spoke softly, but a little desperately. 'The man is here, in Reception.'

'Here?' she echoed with a groan; not only had this man got hold of the name of one of the editors—namely, herself—he had also come here in person. 'Would you—?'

'He's gorgeous, Arabella,' Di continued in that slightly breathless voice. 'Not just good-looking, you understand, but absolutely gorgeous! I—'

'Di.' Arabella halted her, having gone suddenly still, her hand tightly gripping the telephone receiver. 'In what way is he gorgeous?' She impatiently waved her brother to silence as he tried to cut in on the conversation.

'It's a little difficult to say,' Di muttered awkwardly.

Arabella could visualise the receptionist, seated behind her desk, her hand partially over the mouthpiece of the telephone as she attempted to talk to Arabella without alerting the man to what she was actually saying. 'Try,' Arabella prompted; she had no intention of seeing anyone who refused to give even his name. Even if he was, as Di put it, gorgeous!

'Well, he's tall. Really tall,' Di breathed ecstatically, her gaze obviously on the man in question as she spoke. 'With blond hair. A little too long to be fashionable, but on him it looks good. And he has the most amazingly blue eyes. I almost drowned in them when I first looked up at him!' she added.

Arabella's hand had tightened almost painfully about the telephone receiver as Di had described the man's hair, but as the other woman talked of those deep blue eyes, her nails dug into the palm of her hand.

'And he's so good-looking,' Di continued gushingly—obviously well into the subject now. 'But ruggedly so,' she added almost defensively. 'He's just gorgeous, Arabella. In fact,' she added thoughtfully, 'he looks very much like you would expect—'

'Palfrey to look!' Arabella finished forcefully, her face pale now, her eyes wide. There was a huge poster displaying one of the covers of the Palfrey books in Reception, and she could almost imagine Di looking at that poster, then at the man, and seeing the undoubted likeness. Because she had a stomach-plummeting feeling that she knew exactly who the man was in Reception who wanted to see her.

She could also sense Stephen's renewed interest in

the conversation at the mention of Palfrey's name. She kept her gaze firmly averted from him as her thoughts raced; she felt tense enough already, without Stephen adding to it!

'Yes!' Di sounded relieved now that she understood what she was talking about. 'Do you know him?'

Oh, yes, she knew him! But what was Robert Merlin doing here? In the last five years he had refused every invitation she had ever made, asking him to come to London and meet everyone at Atherton Publishing. Now he had simply turned up here uninvited! He was the last person she wanted to see!

But knowing Robert Merlin, even as little as she did, she accepted she wouldn't get away without seeing him. Oh, help!

'Yes, Di, I know him,' she confirmed wearily.

'You do?' The receptionist sounded awed now. 'Will you be—?'

'Arabella, are you saying that Merlin is downstairs?' Stephen burst out incredulously, his curiosity overtaking his good manners.

'Be quiet, Stephen,' Arabella snapped at him tensely. 'I'm talking to Di.'

'But—'

'Yes, I'm saying Robert Merlin is downstairs!' she confirmed for him tautly. 'Now let me talk to Di.' She glared her brother into silence, as he would have spoken again. 'You were saying, Di?' she prompted vaguely, her thoughts still racing. She didn't want to see Robert Merlin. Her embarrassment where he was concerned was so acute, she wasn't sure she would be able to get through such a meeting.

She had made such a fool of herself at his house last week, had somehow let him know how attractive she found him; she had to have done, otherwise why else would he have kissed her in the way he had? 'Engaging in the game of verbal flirtation'. As soon as she had seen the woman to whom he had been married, she'd known exactly how ridiculous the idea of that was!

Now he was here, downstairs. How was she supposed to face him again?

'Will you come down for him, or shall I send him up?' Awe hadn't left the receptionist's voice; Di was obviously impressed that Arabella should know someone so devastatingly attractive.

'Send him up,' Arabella told her quickly, hoping to give herself a little time to compose herself before she had to see him. 'Give him directions to my office. I'll be here waiting for him.' She rang off quickly, before Di could ask any searching questions.

She would be 'waiting for him'! She didn't want to see him. He had no right just turning up in this way. Yet the irony was, she knew that if he had done this before her visit to his house last week she would have been overjoyed.

'Merlin is coming up here?' Stephen sounded as panic-stricken as she felt.

Despite her own feelings, Arabella couldn't help smiling at Stephen's reaction to the arrival of the man who had thrown him off his property ten days ago. 'What's the matter, Stephen?' she taunted. 'A little nervous about meeting him again?'

'"A little nervous" hardly begins to describe it,' Stephen admitted unabashedly. 'I'm not anxious to get on the wrong side of him again!'

Neither was she. But it appeared she had little

choice about seeing him; he was on his way up to her office at this very moment!

'Stephen Atherton, you stop right there!' She halted him as he was about to go out the door. 'Where do you think you're going?' she demanded impatiently, crossing the room to join him.

Her brother shrugged. 'I have some work to do in my own office. I only dropped in to say hello.'

'Well, you can say hello to Robert Merlin, too,' she announced with satisfaction. 'After all, you have to speak to the man again some time,' she pointed out practically.

'"Some time" isn't necessarily now.' He touched her cheek in apology. 'Good luck, sis.' He glanced out into the corridor, grimacing as he did so. 'I have a feeling you're going to need it!'

Arabella felt herself pale as she saw the reason for that grimace; Robert was walking determinedly from the lift in the direction of her office. She had instructed Di to send him up with the intention of giving herself a few minutes' respite to compose herself. He must have come straight up from Reception the second Di finished giving him instructions.

Di was right—he did look gorgeous. Faded blue denims, matched with a pale blue shirt, and a black jacket worn over the latter, added to his rakish air. His over-long hair looked more golden than even against the darkness of his jacket, and his face was tanned from the hours he had spent out in the sunshine—dealing with stubborn tree trunks, no doubt!

'See you later,' Stephen muttered before making good his escape.

'Coward,' she had time to fire back at him before he was out of earshot.

Robert's eyes narrowed as the other man approached on the other side of the carpeted corridor. 'Atherton,' he bit out coldly as they drew level.

'Merlin.' Stephen nodded in greeting just as abruptly, before continuing on to his own office.

Arabella didn't move from the open doorway; what was the point? Robert had already seen her standing there. Besides, she couldn't have moved at that moment anyway; her legs had gone like jelly just at the sight of him!

This wouldn't do at all. She wasn't the same woman who had arrived at his home a week ago—and she didn't just mean in outward appearance. Something had changed in her the moment she'd seen that photograph of Emma's mother and she had felt so despondent because she could never, ever be as beautiful as that woman, could never seriously attract the attention of a man like Robert Merlin.

She had decided then and there that, whilst that was true, it was still no reason not to make the best of herself. It was time she gave up the dream of Palfrey and looked for a real man to love.

So she had gone out and bought herself a whole new wardrobe, of underclothes as well as outer ones, had discarded her glasses in favour of contact lenses—which hadn't proved as difficult to wear as she had thought; in fact she often forgot she was wearing them. The final change had been her hair; a trip to the hairdressers after work yesterday evening had taken care of that. It had been a little like looking at a stranger in the mirror before she'd left for work this morning, but at the same time she'd welcomed the change.

She only hoped her new-found confidence would stand the test of another meeting with Robert Merlin!

'Robert,' she greeted him crisply as he reached her door, that confidence wavering slightly as her brother paused long enough in the doorway of his own office to give her a conspiratorial wink. He wasn't just a coward, he was a damned menace!

Robert stood in front of her, his expression enigmatic as he took in the changes in her appearance. At least, she supposed he'd noticed; he could have taken in so little about the way she looked last week that she seemed no different to him now!

'Arabella,' he returned mockingly.

She stepped back slightly to allow him access to her office. 'You wanted to see me?'

He strode past her into the room, taking his time about answering her as he looked critically around her office.

Arabella followed him, closing the door behind her; it would be just like Stephen, if she left the door ajar, to sneak back and listen outside to their conversation. As she had no idea as to what she owed the honour of this visit, that wasn't an opportunity she intended giving him.

She looked about the room too, trying to see her office through Robert's eyes: the soft peach-coloured walls, the paintings that adorned those walls equally restful, her desk a warm walnut, deep blue carpet on the floor, and several flourishing plants standing in the window and on the walnut filing cabinets along one wall of the room.

It was a restful room, a room she looked forward to entering every day when she came to work. Although she accepted that to Robert it probably looked too comfortably feminine to be a place of work.

He finally turned to look at her, that guarded expression still in his eyes. 'You must tell me who your interior designer is,' he finally drawled. 'Willow House could do with a woman's touch.'

It was difficult to tell from his tone of voice whether he was mocking her or not. Arabella's cheeks were hot with resentment as she answered him. 'I chose all the decor and furnishings in here myself,' she told him tautly.

This had been another concession of her father's when he'd persuaded her to give up her idea of going to university and to come and work at Atherton's instead. Until this moment she had been pleased with her choices...

Robert gave an appreciative nod. 'Then perhaps I should ask you to look at some improvements at Willow House.' As he spoke, he moved to sit in the comfortable leather chair that faced Arabella's, separated by the width of her desk. He was perfectly relaxed as he folded his lean length down into the cream leather, resting the ankle of one leg on the knee of the other as he sat back.

Now she knew he was mocking her!

There was a sparkle of anger in the deep blue of her eyes as she sat down to face him across the desk. 'You wanted to speak to me?' she prompted again, coldly this time.

He looked about him appreciatively once more. 'It's always good to see a person in their own surroundings, don't you think?' he murmured thoughtfully.

Yes, she did think; it was exactly what she had

thought about him last week when she had gone to his home. What she hadn't expected was to be confronted with a living image of Palfrey. But even that was less of a shock to her now; the two men were no longer confused in her mind. Robert might look like Palfrey, but the cynicism in him was nothing like the character in his books: Palfrey was full of humour, with an honourable side to him that came through as a caring for his fellow human beings.

The fact that Robert wrote those books must mean that he, too, possessed those characteristics. But, as he never showed them to the world, it was becoming easier to separate the two men in her mind. It was Palfrey she had fallen in love with; Robert had evoked a physical longing inside her that had hitherto been unknown.

'I'm sure you didn't come all the way to London to pass comment on the decor in my office,' she remarked derisively.

'No,' he conceded lightly. 'Actually I brought Emma up to town.'

Coming here to the publishing house which for the last five years, had published his books had merely been an afterthought!

Was that disappointment she felt? Surely not. Perhaps she hadn't done such a good job of separating the two characters in her mind after all...

His gaze was unwavering as he continued to look at her across the desk. 'Emma wondered if you would like to have lunch with us,' he said quietly.

Emma had wondered, not Robert! 'Why?' She used the same ploy he had used with her a week ago.

But it didn't have the same effect of disconcerting Robert in the way it had her. His shrug was dismissive. 'I don't know; you'll have to ask Emma that. Preferably over lunch,' he added mockingly.

As usual, he was presumptuous. 'I already have an engagement for lunch,' she refused, thankful that it was, in fact, true. She had a feeling Robert would easily be able to tell if she was lying.

He looked at her steadily. 'Then I suggest you break it.'

She drew in a sharp breath. 'I'm afraid that isn't possible.' She managed to keep her voice pleasantly apologetic. But inside she was far from calm; she had known he was difficult, but this amounted to down-right arrogance!

'You left very abruptly last week.'

His sudden change of subject caught her off guard yet again, a blush darkening her cheeks. 'Stella said you were driving Emma to school. I left you a note,' she added defensively.

'I read it,' he acknowledged dryly. '"Thank you for your hospitality. I'll be in touch."' He recited the contents of her note word-perfectly.

Well, let's face it, there wasn't a lot to remember! Mainly because she hadn't had a lot to say. What could she say after the shock she had received in Emma's bedroom on seeing that photograph of her mother? Emma's mother was obviously a subject Robert didn't wish to discuss; he had made that more than obvious when the subject had been raised earlier in the day. He had also made it plain that the subject of filming Palfrey was a no-go area.

In those circumstances, thanking him for dinner and a bed for the night, and stating that she would be in touch with him again once she was back in London,

were the only safe subjects she could put in her brief
note!

'Well, I did. And I have,' she defended dismissively.

'By the latter, I suppose you're referring to this?'
Robert pulled her last letter to him out of the breast
pocket of his jacket.

Arabella's expression became guarded. The fact
that he had the letter with him indicated that his coming here to invite her to join Emma and himself for
lunch hadn't been as casual as he had implied just
now.

Did he know she had seen that photograph in
Emma's bedroom? Had his daughter told him how
shocked she had seemed? How she had quickly made
her excuses to leave Emma's bedroom, to escape?

Arabella could tell nothing of Robert's thoughts
from his expression; he was far too adept at hiding
his feelings.

'I don't require a different editor, Arabella,' he continued in a hard voice, tapping the letter against the
palm of his other hand.

The flush in her cheeks seemed to have become a
permanent fixture, and her movements were flustered.
'Stephen is young, admittedly, and a little impetuous,
perhaps.' She made an effort to excuse the way her
brother had turned up at this man's home uninvited.
'But he's a good editor, gaining in experience all the
time, and—'

'I'm sure your brother is a paragon of virtue—'

'I wouldn't go that far!' Arabella cut in dryly. She
was sure there were several young women of
Stephen's acquaintance who would heartily agree with
her!

'Capable at his job, then,' Robert conceded irritably, his expression grim now. 'I just don't happen to need a different editor; I'm perfectly happy with the one I already have.'

Arabella couldn't meet his probing gaze. Because the truth of the matter was, she was no longer comfortable being this man's editor. Too much had happened that evening at his home for her ever to feel comfortable with him again. And she wasn't just referring to that photograph of his wife.

On her return to London last week, she had written a short, businesslike letter to Robert Merlin, telling him of his change of editor. She had thought he would be happy with the decision.

But she could tell by the harsh expression on his face now that she had thought wrong!

'In the circumstances—'

'What circumstances?' He was watching her with narrowed eyes.

He knew damn well what circumstances. That photograph apart, what had happened between the two of them certainly wasn't normal between an author and their editor!

She drew in a deep, controlling breath, willing her voice to remain placatory. 'I'm sure you would be better off with another editor—'

'I think that is for me to decide,' he cut in harshly. 'Don't you?' he challenged softly.

No, she didn't! She had made this decision because she genuinely didn't believe she could work with him any more. During that single day spent in his company she had ceased to be impartial where he and his work were concerned; she felt too emotionally involved to deal with him on a business level. The best thing for everyone, she thought, was to remove herself from the situation.

She certainly hadn't expected Robert to come here personally and challenge her on the subject!

She had assumed, during the week that had elapsed since she'd sent the letter, that he was happy with the new arrangement too. Now she knew his silence had merely been lulling her into a false sense of security!

'Look, Robert, I—' She broke off as her office door opened without warning. Her father—a man who didn't believe he had to knock on the door of any office in his company—came striding forcefully into the room.

His brows rose slightly as he realised she wasn't alone, but, other than that, he offered no apology for barging in on them the way he had. 'I thought we had a lunch appointment, Arabella?' he reminded her with his usual arrogance.

She was aware of a sudden increase in Robert's interest as he observed the other man, knowing by his totally assessing gaze that he hadn't realised this was her father. It was a natural mistake; there was no apparent similarity between the two to proclaim them father and daughter. But then, the same could be said of Robert and Emma...

'We do,' she confirmed lightly to her father, willing Robert to take the hint to leave now; she didn't want to introduce the two men. It would be better all round if Robert did believe her father was a male friend. And she didn't want her father to realise this was Merlin!

But, as if sensing her unspoken wish, Robert just made himself more comfortable in his chair.

'The matter is settled.' Arabella spoke forcefully to

Robert after several awkward seconds in which no one had spoken at all.

He shook his head. 'Not to my satisfaction.'

His posture clearly said he wasn't about to leave until it was!

She could sense her father's puzzlement, and, knowing him as she did, she knew it wasn't a state of mind he would accept for very long. 'Perhaps we could make an appointment for some other time. One that will suit us both,' she added pointedly, opening the diary that sat on her desk.

Again he shook his head. 'I'm only in London until tomorrow morning.'

For the moment, he wasn't about to budge; his tone clearly told her that. She was at a loss to know what to say to him next.

'What seems to be the problem here?' Her father, predictably, had become impatient with the enigmatic conversation, and had clearly had enough of waiting for Arabella to join him.

'The problem,' Robert chose to answer before Arabella could do so, 'seems to be that Arabella has double-booked herself for lunch today.' His gaze openly challenged her as he made the arrogant statement.

Because he knew damn well she had never agreed to have lunch with him—the opposite, in fact! But she knew by her father's frown that he believed the other man. Why shouldn't he? What possible reason could Robert have for saying such a thing if it wasn't true? What indeed!

She stood up, deciding it was time she took charge of this situation before it spiralled out of control any further. Besides, she knew now that, whatever she might have hoped earlier, there was no way she was going to get away with not introducing the two men. That was too much to hope for!

'Father, this is our author Merlin—Robert Merlin. Robert, my father, Martin Atherton.' She might not have wanted to make the introduction, but she knew a moment's satisfaction when they each looked disconcerted by the identity of the other.

If Robert hadn't even begun to imagine this tall, distinguished man might be her father, then she could see that Robert had come as even more of a surprise to her father!

She had said little about Robert when she had returned home last week, merely confirming to her father and Stephen that she too had failed to persuade Merlin to agree to the making of a Palfrey film. Their joint I-told-you-so looks had been mild compared to the ridicule she would have been subjected to if they had known that not only had she failed to persuade Merlin, but she had also fallen in love with the man!

'Mr Merlin.' Her father recovered rapidly, holding out his hand to the other man in greeting, now in charming mode, as Arabella had thought he might be. 'So nice to meet you at long last,' he added smoothly, not revealing by a word or a gesture the arrogant assertions he had made last week concerning this man and the publishing house.

'Atherton.' Robert returned the handshake, but guardedly—almost as if he were well aware of the way her father had been so derogatory about him the previous week.

Her father's eyes were narrowed thoughtfully. 'And you say that you and Arabella have a luncheon appointment?'

Robert gave her another challenging glance before turning back to the older man. 'We do,' he confirmed abruptly.

'Well, in the circumstances, Arabella, of course you must go to lunch with Mr Merlin.' Again her father was predictable—he knew damn well she didn't have a previous lunch appointment, with this man or anybody else.

Because she had confirmed after consulting her business diary not more than an hour ago that she was free to lunch with her father!

But obviously her father saw a chance: because this man had come here, perhaps she would be successful today, as she hadn't been the previous week, where the Palfrey film was concerned. The thought of all that money for Atherton Publishing was by far a bigger incentive to her father than having lunch with the daughter he saw every day!

There was no way out of this now, she could see that—not without making a complete fool of herself, and embarrassing her father.

A fact she knew, by the triumphant glitter in his eyes, that Robert was well aware of!

CHAPTER SIX

'WHEN did you cut your hair?'

At last! She had begun to think Robert hadn't noticed. Her father hadn't. She had left early for the office today, before her father and Stephen, and she had been out on a date with Malcolm last night. Stephen had at least noticed earlier.

Part of the furniture, came to her mind.

She wondered when her father had last looked at her and actually seen Arabella, the woman. Perhaps never, she realised sadly. She had always just been there, good old Arabella, ensuring that his home ran smoothly. Apart from that he had no reason to notice her, she accepted.

Malcolm had been highly attentive the previous evening. He had even suggested they meet again tonight. It was an invitation Arabella had had no trouble refusing. Malcolm might find her new look more attractive, but her feelings towards him hadn't changed in the least; he was an amusing occasional companion, but, after seeing him on that basis for the last three months, she didn't think her feelings for him were going to deepen now.

Oh, he was attractive and amusing enough, and last night he had left her in no doubt as to how much he desired her. But he wasn't Palfrey!

Neither was the man seated beside her in the taxi going to the restaurant to meet Emma. He wasn't even

Merlin, she knew now. She had to keep remembering that.

'Some time ago,' she answered him dismissively.

'It's only been a week since I last saw you,' Robert returned mockingly.

'Really?' She fixed a cool blue gaze on him. 'I wasn't counting.'

His mouth quirked at her sarcasm. 'Would it surprise you to learn that I was?' He arched his brows questioningly.

'Playing the verbal flirtation game again, Robert?' she taunted.

He turned in his seat to look at her more closely, his knee lightly touching hers now. 'It seems not only the hairstyle has changed in the last week,' he murmured thoughtfully.

She had made a fool of herself with this man a week ago; she had known that as soon as she'd seen the photograph of Emma's mother. Robert was right—she had changed in the last week; she had grown up, stopped looking for Palfrey. Because he simply didn't exist. Not even in this man, who looked so much like Palfrey.

'It suits you, Arabella.' Robert lightly touched the fiery red tendrils of hair against her cheek.

She knew that, had been delighted herself with the result last night when the hairdresser had shown her the style from all angles in a mirror. It gave her a sophisticated air, emphasised the size of her eyes, gave her face an elfin beauty she had never seen before. And it had been obvious, from his more ardent attitude the previous evening, that Malcolm appreciated her new look.

Now this man seemed equally appreciative.

She slid further along the bench seat towards the taxi door, Robert's hand falling away from her cheek, his knee no longer touching hers. 'Thank you,' she accepted stiltedly. 'Why did you say Emma came to London?' She changed the subject abruptly, and knew from the way Robert's mouth tightened that it was something he wasn't happy talking about.

She had only been making conversation, keeping it safely away from herself. Was there any subject the two of them could talk about that didn't cause one or both displeasure? The weather probably! Although they probably wouldn't even agree on that; she loved the cold and snow, too much sunshine bringing out her freckles and burning her pale skin, but from the look of Robert's deeply tanned skin he loved the sun!

'I didn't say,' he bit out tersely, a closed expression on his face.

End of subject, Arabella guessed ruefully. Yet another topic they couldn't talk about. Well, that suited Arabella just fine—because she had nothing to say about his change of editor either! Two could play at this game!

She turned to look pointedly out of the window. 'The weather is nice for this time of year,' she broached, testing yet another theory, and turned back towards Robert as she heard him chuckle. 'Did I say something funny?' She raised her auburn brows.

He still smiled; his face was softer than she had ever seen it, his eyes warm, with laughter-lines at their sides, and his teeth very white and even as he grinned at her. 'Truce, Arabella?' He held out his hand in a friendly gesture.

She stared at that hand, remembering the way he had stroked her cheek minutes ago; she still felt the warmth against her skin. She still found him attractive, still reacted to his touch.

'I don't bite, Arabella,' he encouraged huskily as she made no move to take hold of his hand.

As she continued to stare at his hand she imagined him nibbling the tips of her fingers, the lobes of her ears, the base of her throat. She closed her eyes to shut out the sensual vision. But that only made it more intense; a shiver of awareness ran down her spine as she could almost feel his lips against her breasts—

Stop! She had to stop these flights of fantasy every time she was in this man's company.

'Do you think the weather is nice for this time of year?' she prompted abruptly.

He shrugged. 'As late springs go, this one is—nice?' He grimaced at her questioningly.

Now it was Arabella's turn to chuckle. 'Perhaps we should mark this one down in our diaries: "Arabella and Robert agreed about something"!' she reflected ruefully as he continued to look at her.

'I'm sure we could agree on a lot of things, if we really tried,' Robert said huskily.

He was still playing with her, and no matter what he might assume to the contrary, after the way she had responded in his arms the previous week, she did not go in for casual flings. Not even with Merlin, who had turned out to be the man of her dreams, a modern-day Palfrey!

'We appear to have differing opinions concerning your new editor,' she reminded him briskly.

'Not different at all, Arabella,' he dismissed easily. 'I accept that your brother is more than capable; I just don't happen to be in need of a new editor.'

'That wasn't the impression I gained last week,' she

said sharply. 'Then I had the distinct feeling you would have preferred A. Atherton to be a man!'

Robert shrugged. 'That was last week.'

Nothing had changed in the interim period, as far as Arabella was concerned, to make his reaction any more acceptable. In fact, the opposite!

She drew in a ragged breath. 'The truth is, Robert, that I'm no longer happy with the direction the Palfrey books are taking.'

His mouth twisted mockingly. 'They aren't taking a "direction", Arabella; they're finishing!'

'Exactly,' she acknowledged tautly.

Dark blond brows rose over cold blue eyes. 'Do you try to tell other authors how to write their books?'

'Sometimes I—guide them in the right direction.' She chose her words carefully, for, in truth, she only did so when specifically asked by an author—if he or she had become bogged down by the storyline, or had writer's block.

But the Palfrey books were too personal to her, and she quite simply didn't feel she was the right editor to deal with the character's demise; it would be like aiding the death of a dearly beloved friend.

'I don't need guidance, Arabella—'

'I disagree!' she cut in vehemently. 'You see...' she sighed as she realised how emotional she had sounded '...this simply isn't going to work any more.' She shook her head determinedly.

Robert was watching her. 'Why don't you wait until after you've read the last Palfrey manuscript before making any decision on this?' he encouraged lightly.

Her stomach gave a sickening lurch just hearing those words 'the last Palfrey manuscript'!

She didn't ever want to read it, because if she didn't

Palfrey would stay alive in her memory. In fact, she was starting to dislike this man who sat at her side, because he was the one instrumental in killing Palfrey...

'No,' she told him unrelentingly. 'Where are we meeting Emma?' She changed the subject abruptly. Emma was something they could agree on, because Arabella liked the young girl's candour and lack of affectation, and Robert was obviously very proud of his daughter.

He looked at her wordlessly for several moments, and then he gave a slight nod, as if inwardly accepting her prevarication. For the moment. Arabella didn't doubt he would return to the issue some other time.

But her answer would still be the same. Over this she was adamant. There was no room for negotiation. She would not edit the book in which he killed Palfrey.

'A quiet little restaurant that does wonderful pasta, and which not too many people seem to have discovered as yet,' he said in answer to her question. 'Emma and I always go there when we're in London.'

Why wasn't she surprised to learn he preferred to frequent a restaurant 'not too many people' had 'discovered'?

'And do you come up to London often?' she prompted conversationally.

'Often enough,' he returned guardedly—almost as if he suspected her reason for asking.

But there wasn't one! She was literally just making conversation. But it seemed that every subject she broached was fraught with tension. The best thing would be if she didn't say anything at all!

So she didn't, concentrating on the passing streets as they were driven to the unknown restaurant.

Except that it wasn't!

She began to realise, as they drove through streets very close to the home she shared with her father and brother, exactly which restaurant they were going to!

Mario's was a trattoria she and her family went to often; in fact one of the dishes on the menu, Spaghetti Arabella, was actually named for her—because for the first six months when she had visited the restaurant she had ordered the same delicious spaghetti dish. It had become so that she didn't even have to make her order any more; Mario just brought the dish for her automatically. She had blushed with embarrassment— and a lot of pleasure—when she'd seen the menu had been changed to name the dish after her.

But in all the times she had visited the restaurant she was sure she had never seen Robert or Emma there; she would have remembered them if she had. So probably 'often enough' meant very infrequently.

Arabella couldn't help smiling to herself as she wondered what Robert was going to say when Mario greeted her, as he usually did, like a long-lost relative—even if she had only visited the restaurant the week before.

The smells that greeted one on entering the dimly lit, homely restaurant were enough to make one's mouth water, and, as Arabella knew from years of experience, the food more than lived up to that initial promise of excellence.

Arabella knew exactly what Robert had meant when he'd said not too many people had discovered the restaurant yet; it wasn't frequented by the fashionable crowd, probably being a little too far from the main streets of London.

But, as usual, today it was busy with regular lunchtime workers from nearby offices, the food being good and inexpensive enough for them to make this a regular treat. Mario and his staff were always welcoming. To be in Mario's restaurant was to feel as if you were part of a very large family.

'Emma's already here,' Robert remarked at her side. 'She's sitting—'

'Arabella! *Bambina!*' Mario smiled from ear to ear as soon as he saw her. He was in his early fifties, barely over five feet high, almost as round as he was tall, and was wearing his usual white shirt and black trousers, with a large white apron secured about his waist; his hair was jet-black, a narrow moustache on his top lip giving him a rakish air. He looked like a typical Italian from films. '*Bellissima—*'

'Speak English, Mario, if you intend to go on flattering me,' Arabella cut in with dry affection. 'I may as well enjoy it, and you know I don't speak a word of Italian!' She also knew that he was quickly running out of things to say in his own language, because he had been born in East London—and had the accent to match!

In fact, he had once confided in her that he had never actually seen his grandparents' native country, and, being a second generation immigrant, knew little of the language either. But luckily for all of his customers his parents had passed on their skills in Italian cooking!

'You look beautiful with the new hair.' He spoke in the accented English he knew his customers expected, although privately he lapsed into the broadest

Cockney Arabella had ever heard! 'Roberto!' He had spotted the man standing just slightly apart from and behind her in the entrance. 'Two of my favourite people arriving together!' He beamed at them both, his moustache seeming to reach from ear to ear, shaking Robert's hand with the great enthusiasm he seemed to give to most things.

'We've arrived together because we are together, Mario,' Robert told him dryly, obviously a little bemused by the whole encounter.

'You are together?' Mario forgot his accented English in his surprise. 'Well, I—But—This eesa wonderful!' The accent returned as he quickly gathered himself together. 'I will give you both my best table—'

'Emma is already seated at it, Mario,' Robert cut in derisively.

The proprietor glanced round to where Emma sat, the young girl giving them a wave of acknowledgement.

'At least,' Robert added mockingly, 'that's what you told me the last time we were here!'

'But it is.' Mario had recovered completely now. 'Come, I will take you to her.' He moved his heavy bulk through the tables; as with most heavy people, he was quite light on his feet.

'So much for my little Italian restaurant that not too many people seem to have discovered as yet!' Robert muttered behind her self-derisively.

Arabella glanced back at him. 'Don't feel too bad,' she cajoled. 'In the main I think you're probably right; I just happen to have been coming here for years. Our family home isn't too far from here,' she added by way of explanation.

'It's your "local", so to speak?' he said wryly.

Arabella thought of the large family house that overlooked the park, exclusive in its locality—and price. Not that her father would ever consider selling; it had belonged to the eldest Atherton son for generations, and no doubt would pass on to her brother and his wife some day. Arabella quickly put from her mind what would happen to her then.

'Something like that,' she confirmed evasively. 'Mario, this is a business lunch,' she cautioned as he miraculously produced two of the candles that were usually only put onto the tables at night, and proceeded to light them.

'Business?' He looked startled, hesitating in putting his lighter to the second candle, one already glowing romantically.

'Business,' she echoed firmly. 'I don't—'

'Light the candle, Mario,' Robert requested of the other man dryly. 'I need all the help I can get!'

Emma chuckled as Arabella's cheeks heated with a mixture of anger and embarrassment. 'Lovely to see you again, Arabella,' she greeted her warmly. 'And your hair looks great,' she enthused, face aglow with welcome. 'I had a feeling it would.'

'Another one of your "feelings", Emma?' her father teased lightly, sitting down himself after holding back Arabella's chair for her. 'And just when did you have this one?' He arched questioning brows as Mario departed, leaving them time to look at the menus.

'Last week at home, when I was waiting to escort Arabella down to dinner,' Emma supplied dismissively before turning back to Arabella. 'You have beautiful eyes, too,' she told her enthusiastically.

'You were completely wrong about that duckling, Arabella.' She gave a happy smile.

'I don't see duckling on the menu.' Robert frowned his puzzlement.

Emma and Arabella shared a conspiratorial laugh, Arabella inwardly pleased by the young girl's effusive compliments.

'But I do see Spaghetti Arabella?'

She laughed again—mainly at the self-derisive expression on Robert's face. 'I cannot tell a lie...'

'It seems, Emma, that we have inadvertently stumbled upon Arabella's favourite restaurant,' he acknowledged ruefully.

They were—also inadvertently—talking about something they didn't disagree on! Amazing! Also unnerving. It had been easier to cope with seeing Robert again when they were antagonists.

But it was hard to keep up the animosity between them when Emma was present, with her bubbly enthusiasm for everything. The young girl even insisted they all had to order Spaghetti Arabella, in honour of the fact that they were dining with its namesake.

'The main ingredient in the spaghetti is seafood,' Arabella told them with a frown. 'So if you don't like seafood—'

'We love it!' Emma interrupted her. 'Don't we, Daddy?' she prompted eagerly.

'Apparently,' he said dryly, putting down his menu to give their order to Mario; the proprietor waited on them himself, 'in honour of the occasion', as he so embarrassingly put it.

'And a bottle of my best red wine.' Mario beamed at them. 'On the 'ouse. In honour—'

'Of the occasion,' Robert finished for him. 'If you insist, Mario,' he accepted ruefully.

'Oh, I do.' The portly man continued to smile at them widely. 'I've known Arabella since she was—a long time,' he amended as she frowned at him. 'But she never bring a man here with her before. And now she bring you, of all the men that she—'

'Actually, Mario, if we're going to be exact about this, Robert brought me,' Arabella cut in uncomfortably; the last thing she wanted was Mario giving Robert the impression that in all the years he had known her she had never been close to a man. Even if she hadn't been involved deeply enough with one to bring him to the restaurant she frequented so often! Stephen was her regular escort, both of them loving Italian food, and Mario's certainly was good!

'Where is Stephen today?' Mario seemed to read her thoughts. ''E will be upset to have missed lunch; the bolognese is especially good today.'

'I'll tell him,' Arabella assured him, wishing Mario would just go away now. She was very fond of him, but he did have a habit of talking too much. She would rather he didn't do so about her private life in front of Robert Merlin!

As if in answer to her wish, Mario left to give their order to the kitchen, Arabella heaving an inward sigh of relief as he did so.

'Stephen?' Emma queried interestedly.

Arabella turned to answer her. 'Stephen is my younger brother—'

'The young man I asked to leave last week,' Robert reminded Emma, at the same time glancing mockingly at Arabella.

Emma's eyes widened. 'I think "asked to leave" is rather an understatement on your part, Daddy!'

'And I think that it may be a little presumptuous on our part to assume there isn't some other man in Arabella's life, just because of Mario's comment,' her father returned dryly.

Arabella felt her cheeks begin to burn again as father and daughter looked at her with the same expression of curiosity. 'Very presumptuous,' she finally muttered uncomfortably.

Robert raised dark blond brows. 'Does that mean there is a man, or there isn't, or that it's just none of our business?'

Arabella looked at him searchingly. Why did he want to know? Why show such interest in the first place in that part of Mario's conversation?

She could read nothing from his sardonic expression. 'Yes,' she answered unhelpfully.

His eyes narrowed, and his emotion was easy to read this time—it was displeasure! 'Just what does that mean?' he said harshly.

'It means,' Emma answered him with a grin, 'that there is a man, possibly even a couple of men, but there's no one serious.'

Arabella gave the young girl a surprised look; she could see she would have to be more careful in future of what she said in front of Emma. In future? There weren't going to be any future meetings, with any member of the Merlin family!

Robert turned to his daughter, a slight frown marring his brow now. 'How did you deduce that? Not another one of your "feelings"?' he mocked lightly.

'Not really.' Emma sat back, warming to her subject now. 'But if there was a man Arabella was serious about, or even an engagement, then she wouldn't be so cagey about it. Besides, no ring,' she added, with a knowing look at Arabella's bare left hand.

Arabella only just resisted the impulse to put that telling bare left hand down in her lap, beneath the table. Emma was too devious for her own good. And Arabella's! And she had thought the young girl quite liked her!

'But you still think there is a man?' Robert was also warming to the subject, but for quite another reason; he was enjoying watching Arabella squirm! 'Of sorts?' he added insultingly, giving Arabella a look of sweeping humour.

At her expense! Really, these two were far too fond of conducting conversations that caused her embarrassment.

'Mmm.' Emma nodded with certainty.

'Just why do you think that?' her father asked.

'Because Arabella is far too beautiful for there not to be!' Emma told him with satisfaction.

Now it was Arabella's turn to smile. Good old Emma; she was still her friend, after all.

'Very "elementary, my dear Watson",' her father said disgustedly. 'I—Here comes our food.' He had looked up as Mario bustled his way over to their table, somehow balancing the three plates in his hands, plus a basket of garlic bread. 'In the nick of time, wouldn't you say?' Robert leant forward to say this quietly for Arabella's ears alone.

She didn't say anything, studiously avoiding so much as even looking at him again as the three of them began their meal. As usual, it was delicious.

She turned to Emma. 'Have you enjoyed your day in London shopping?' she said conversationally.

'Er-yes.' Emma glanced quickly at her father. 'There's nowhere quite like London for shopping, is there?' she dismissed brightly.

'Nowhere,' Arabella agreed distractedly, also looking at Robert. There was something not quite right here, but she could see that neither father nor daughter was about to enlighten her.

She returned to concentrating on her meal, her appreciation completely genuine when Mario came to check on them a few minutes later.

'Yes, it's excellent, Mario.' Robert added his praise. 'Almost as lovely as its namesake,' he tacked on with self-mockery once Mario had happily gone on his way.

'Daddy!' Emma groaned, rolling her eyes with feeling. 'That was really corny!'

He shrugged dismissively. 'It's been a while; I'm a little out of practice.'

'A lot out of practice,' Emma agreed affectionately. 'Palfrey would have done much better.'

'I'm sure he would,' Robert accepted dryly. 'At that moment Arabella would have melted into his arms.' He was eyeing her mockingly again now. 'But then, I'm not Palfrey,' he added softly.

No, he certainly wasn't! If only she could separate the two in her mind, but unfortunately that was becoming more and more difficult...

'I'm not going to melt into anyone's arms!' she returned sharply.

Again, she could have added. Because she had certainly melted in this man's arms once before.

Was it her imagination, or did he mutter 'Pity' beneath his breath...?

She must have imagined it, because now he seemed to be completely engrossed in eating his food.

Whereas Arabella was having trouble eating hers. That would never do; Mario would never forgive her. She—'It seems your father has someone to share lunch with him after all,' Robert said slowly at her side.

Arabella looked up sharply, frowning at Robert, following the direction of his gaze—just in time to see her father being shown to a table across the room from them. With him was a very beautiful blonde. She was the obvious reason for Robert's remark.

The woman looked quite young, possibly five or six years older than Arabella, with straight blonde hair to her shoulders, her fringe emphasising the depth of her green eyes. She was wearing a short black sheath of a dress that finished just above her knees, and her legs were long and shapely, despite the fact she only looked to be a little over five feet in height.

The woman was beautiful; Arabella's father obviously thought so too, as he was very solicitous as he pulled out her chair for her, before taking his own seat. Their two heads were soon bent very close together as they looked at a single menu, one so golden blonde, the other much darker and peppered with grey.

'Very nice,' Robert drawled appreciatively. 'A friend of the family?'

'No,' Arabella snapped, turning away from the engrossed couple. 'I've never seen her before.' She didn't particularly care for the fact that Robert obviously shared her father's opinion that the woman was very beautiful. As she had already guessed, Robert was attracted to very beautiful women, if his wife and her father's companion were anything to go by.

She was jealous. One hundred per cent green-eyed jealous!

Thankfully, Robert was still watching the couple and didn't see her dismay at the realisation. 'Your father seems to know her quite well,' he mused.

Arabella had realised that in her first sweeping glance. But she was sure she had never seen the woman before, and she very much doubted that her brother had either—Stephen would have mentioned it if he had.

So who was she? Why hadn't her father told either herself or Stephen about this latest woman in his life? He wasn't usually so careful of his privacy. More importantly, why had her father chosen this particular restaurant? He had intended taking Arabella to a rather more fashionable one in town.

Oh, why was she the one who felt so uncomfortable at seeing him with this unknown woman...?

'Do you think your mother knows about her?' Robert said slowly, his gaze narrowed as he watched the familiarity between the couple seated across the room.

Arabella turned to him with widely indignant eyes. 'My mother has been dead for fifteen years!'

'Oh.' He frowned. 'Sorry. But from your reaction at seeing them together just now I thought maybe—'

'Well, don't,' she snapped. 'My father is perfectly at liberty to see whomever he chooses!'

'Fine.' Robert held up his hands apologetically. 'Don't you think perhaps you ought to go over and say hello?' he prompted lightly.

Should she? The fact was, she didn't want to. But

she didn't feel she had a choice, not with Robert and Emma sitting here looking at her so curiously.

'Yes,' she conceded heavily, standing up reluctantly and placing her checked napkin carefully on the table-top. 'I shouldn't be long.' Not if she could help it! How embarrassing this all was. She wasn't at all sure her father was going to be pleased to see her here either; he had never made any secret in the past about the woman he was seeing, and yet this time he hadn't mentioned a thing...

The two were deeply engrossed in conversation as Arabella approached their table. She was almost upon them when her father glanced up and saw her. To say he looked startled was an understatement; there was a look almost of guilt on his face as he stood up abruptly.

'Arabella!' His voice was too loud in its forced joviality. 'My dear. We were just talking about you...' he added lamely.

Were they, indeed? Well, that was more than he had done with her about his luncheon companion! 'Something nice, I hope?' Her own uncomfortable smile encompassed them both.

'Martin is always singing your praises, Arabella.' The female companion was the one to answer, smiling up at her father affectionately. 'He was just explaining to me that, because of your work commitments, he was suddenly free to take me to lunch instead.'

'But Alison,' Arabella's father protested, 'you know I—'

'I'm sure Martin wasn't as uncomplimentary as that,' Robert was the one to put in soothingly. This was the first indication Arabella had of him having accompanied her to her father's table! 'In fact,' he added lightly, 'he's probably as happy as I am that I stole Arabella away for lunch.' As he spoke, he curved a proprietorial hand about Arabella's elbow.

Arabella froze defensively, not caring for that almost possessive clasp on her arm. But to move away from him would look too pointed.

'I'm Robert Merlin.' He held out his free hand to the woman seated at the table.

The green eyes were dark with warmth as she shook that hand. 'Alison Wilder,' she supplied huskily.

The name was no help whatsoever to Arabella; she still had no idea who the woman was. Her father still looked decidedly uncomfortable about the whole encounter!

She found her own hand being shaken by Alison Wilder next. 'Arabella Atherton,' she supplied automatically. 'But then—' she frowned across at her father '—you already know that...'

Her father wasn't meeting her gaze, deliberately so, adding to her puzzlement over this situation. He had never been in the least embarrassed about his relationships in the past... What did it mean?

'I would ask the two of you to join us,' Robert continued lightly, 'but, as we have almost finished our meal, and you're just about to start...' He shrugged dismissively.

'Quite. Quite,' Arabella's father agreed with forced joviality. 'Well...don't let us keep you,' he added pointedly as they made no move to leave.

'Martin!' Alison admonished in light rebuke.

'I—er—meant from your charming companion, of course,' he excused effusively.

'Emma is my daughter,' Robert supplied dryly.

Arabella's father glanced across the room at the

young girl, a slight frown on his forehead. 'She's lovely,' he said slowly.

'Thank you,' Robert accepted dismissively. 'And you're right—we really should be on our way—'

'I didn't mean it quite like that, Merlin,' Arabella's father grumbled uncomfortably.

'Neither did I.' Robert was obviously enjoying himself—at the other man's expense. 'But I need to get back to trying to persuade your stubborn daughter that she really does want to continue being my editor after all!'

Arabella gave an inward groan—she couldn't give an outward one because that would have let Robert know just how much of a point he had scored with that statement. Because now it was her turn to be unable to meet her father's searching gaze!

'Is there some doubt about it?' her father asked Robert,—although his eyes remained firmly fixed on Arabella.

Robert was watching the two of them. 'There appears to be...' he said slowly.

'In what way?' her father demanded tartly, his mouth a thin, disapproving line.

'I shouldn't worry about it, Atherton,' Robert told him dismissively. 'I'm sure I'll be able to talk Arabella round.'

She glared at him. He had no intention of 'talking her round'; he was making sure right now, by talking about it in front of her father, that he got his own way. Her father looked absolutely furious at the disclosure!

He nodded abruptly now. 'Let me know if you don't,' he bit out harshly.

'Oh, I will,' Robert nodded. 'I hope you enjoy your meal.' He spoke lightly to Alison Wilder.

'I'm sure I will,' she accepted smoothly.

'Try the Spaghetti Arabella,' he advised mockingly. 'It's delicious!'

Its namesake was absolutely livid as they walked back to the table to rejoin Emma.

How had Robert guessed that her father hadn't any knowledge, as yet, of her decision not to edit Merlin's books any longer? Because he had known somehow—and had deliberately used the conversation just now to put her in an awkward position. Oh, she had intended telling her father—of course she had; it would have been impossible not to. But she would have told him in her own way, in her own time. And the way that Robert Merlin had told him had not allowed that!

Her father would never tolerate such a major decision being made without consulting him. In the circumstances, Arabella knew he would insist that she continue to be Robert Merlin's editor.

She was sure that Robert had been well aware of that when he'd instigated the conversation!

CHAPTER SEVEN

ARABELLA'S mouth was tight, her eyes flashing with fire as she resumed her seat at the table. Robert Merlin was a manipulative, conniving—

'Did I say something wrong?' he asked innocently—too innocently!—as he too sat down.

She glared at him furiously, her breasts quickly rising and falling with anger. 'You know damn well you did,' she snapped tautly.

'Daddy?' Emma looked worried by the unmistakable tension emanating from Arabella. 'What have you done?'

'I have no idea.' He gave a puzzled shake of his head—and all the time his eyes were gently mocking Arabella!

He knew exactly what he had done! Knew it, and found it all rather amusing. She had no doubt her father would have quite a lot to say the next time he saw her.

'Anyone for dessert?' Robert continued brightly. 'Perhaps you could recommend something, Arabella?'

She didn't know about recommend—but she would certainly like to tell him what he could do with the dessert. And his books! 'I never eat dessert,' she muttered in answer to both questions.

'Sweet enough already?'

Arabella had known she had given him the opening almost as soon as she'd made her remark, but by that time it was too late to go back on it. She should have known he would take the opportunity!

Emma groaned beside her. 'That was even worse than the last compliment you tried to give Arabella!'

'Were they compliments?' Arabella said scornfully, still angry. 'I had no idea!'

Emma giggled as her father frowned darkly; she was obviously enjoying the exchange.

'It's as well your father has always shunned publicity,' Arabella continued scathingly, warming to her subject now. 'I wouldn't care to do his PR on a book-signing tour!' She met his gaze challengingly.

He gave a dismissive shrug. 'Just as well it will never happen, then—because I would make a point of asking for you!'

'He would too.' Emma grimaced. 'Just to be awkward.'

Arabella knew that—and he would probably get her!

She made a point of looking at her watch, and was genuinely surprised to see it was almost two o'clock. 'I really should get back to the office now,' she told them lightly. 'Especially as my father doesn't look as if he intends returning for some time,' she added abruptly. Her father and Alison were still deeply engrossed in their conversation, their first course just arriving at their table.

'Alison seems very nice,' Robert put in softly.

Her mouth tightened. Of course Alison seemed nice; she was very beautiful. Not dark, as Robert's wife had been, but with a blonde Nordic beauty. Robert was sure to find her attractive.

'Very,' she acknowledged tersely. 'I really do have to go now. Please do stay on and have dessert and coffee,' she added in a businesslike manner. 'Atherton Publishing has an account here.'

'I invited you out to lunch, Arabella,' Robert rasped harshly. 'Which means I pick up the bill at the end of it.'

Arabella was about to protest, but one look at the coldness of his face told her that wouldn't be advisable. 'As you wish.' She shrugged before turning to smile warmly at Emma. 'It was lovely to see you again. Thank you for thinking of me,' she added warmly, her liking of the young girl completely genuine.

'You notice she didn't include me in any of that.' Robert arched his brows as he addressed the remark to his daughter.

'I seem to remember you said it was Emma's idea to invite me to lunch?' she reminded him tauntingly.

'Is that what he told you?' Emma gave her father a teasing look.

Robert held her gaze steadily. 'That's what I told her,' he confirmed evenly.

Emma looked at him consideringly for several seconds, and then she shrugged dismissively. 'Then it must be true.' She turned to Arabella. 'Daddy doesn't tell lies.'

Maybe he hadn't in the past, but Arabella had a definite feeling he had this time—which begged the question, why had he wanted her to come out to lunch with him today? Even more puzzling, why pretend it was Emma's idea?

She stood up to leave. 'Well, I enjoyed the meal. No matter who the invitation came from,' she added ruefully.

Robert looked up at her. 'How about the company? Did you enjoy that too?'

Strangely enough, until the last few minutes, when her father and Alison had arrived, she had been enjoying herself. On her own with him, she was still terrified of the physical reaction Robert evoked, but with Emma present too the tension tended to be defused, Emma teasing her father in a way Arabella had never yet dared to. Yet? She would never tease Robert in that way, probably wouldn't see him again after today.

She nodded slowly. 'I enjoyed that too,' she admitted huskily.

Robert stood up too, instantly towering over her. 'I'll walk you out to a taxi.'

She didn't argue with him, knowing at that moment it would be useless to do so. Giving Emma a wave goodbye, she felt her arm taken in that proprietorial grasp once again as Robert guided her through the crowded restaurant. She glanced briefly round at her father's table, but as he was still deeply engrossed in conversation with Alison she didn't bother to say goodbye to him. After all, she had no doubt she would see him again all too quickly!

'I hope your father doesn't give you a hard time.' Robert seemed to read her thoughts.

Arabella turned to give him a scathing glance as they went out onto the pavement. 'Do you?'

He clasped both her arms as he turned her to face him. 'I want you to continue as my editor, Arabella,' he said grimly.

She gave a rueful grimace. 'By fair means or foul?' she taunted.

His mouth tightened. 'If necessary, yes,' he ground out harshly, his hands tightening on her arms.

Arabella looked up at him—she couldn't seem to do anything else! At that moment they might have been the only two people on earth as far as she was concerned; Arabella saw no one but Robert. 'Why?' Her voice was huskily soft.

For an answer Robert bent his head and gently claimed her lips with his own, crushing her body forcefully against his, while his mouth continued that sensual plunder. Both of them were breathless when Robert finally raised his head to look into her face, his eyes a deep, misty blue. Di was right—they were eyes to drown in!

'Because it's what I want, Arabella,' he told her gruffly, still holding her tightly against him.

She swallowed hard, not knowing if she could still speak. 'Do you always get what you want?' Her voice was barely above a whisper, but she could still speak!

He gave an impatient shake of his head. 'Not very often, no,' he acknowledged harshly. 'This I happen to want more than most things,' he admitted grimly.

Her breathing was shallow, her mouth dry as she moistened her lips with the tip of her tongue. Before she realised Robert's gaze was locked on the movement, and knew how provocative she must look. 'Why?' she said again; the words forced themselves past the dryness of her throat now.

'Because I very much want you to read the last Palfrey book, Arabella,' he told her urgently. 'I—'

He wanted her to read the book in which Palfrey died!

She pulled away from him, her breathing ragged now. 'Submit the manuscript when it's ready, Robert,' she bit out tensely. 'And I guarantee it will be read.' But not by her. She didn't care what her father had to say on the subject; she would not edit that particular book.

Robert looked at her searchingly. 'But not by you.' He correctly guessed her thoughts.

Arabella went to flag down a passing taxi, grateful when—by some miracle—the first one she put her hand out to actually pulled over to the side of the road. 'I have to go, Robert.' She didn't answer his statement. 'Once again, thank you for lunch.'

She felt rather silly as she realised she had automatically held out her hand to shake his in parting, letting her arm drop limply back to her side as Robert gave her a look that told her he too thought it ridiculous in the circumstances!

'I hope you and Emma enjoy the rest of your stay in London.' She had the taxi door open ready to get in now, the driver waiting patiently.

To get in? To run would be more like it! She had to be away from this man; she had felt herself being drawn under his spell once again. Until he had mentioned Palfrey...

'We will,' he accepted dismissively, his expression grim. 'Arabella—'

'I really do have to go, Robert,' she said quickly. 'Take care,' she told him as she got hastily inside the taxi and closed the door firmly behind her. Unfortunately the window had been left down because of the warmth of the day.

'You too, Arabella.' Robert spoke to her through that open window. 'We'll meet again,' he told her softly as she leant forward to give the taxi driver her destination.

She didn't answer Robert, her gaze fixed steadily ahead as the taxi moved out into the flow of traffic. They wouldn't meet again. She didn't care what her father chose to say to her; she couldn't be with Robert Merlin again. Under any circumstances.

'Partings are always like that, aren't they, love?' The driver spoke to her from his cab at the front of the vehicle. 'Always sad. But I shouldn't cry; he did say he would see you again,' he encouraged in a friendly tone.

Crying...? Who was crying?

She was! She could feel the hot tears on her cheeks now, taste their salt when she licked the moisture from her lips.

Who was she crying for? Herself? Robert? Or was it Palfrey? She simply didn't know any more...

'Just what did you think you were doing, Arabella?' her father demanded, having arrived home a short time ago, his first whisky of the evening already in his hand.

She looked up from polishing the silver, a job she always did herself, as she sat in the dining-room. She had always found the job therapeutic, especially when, as often in the past, she had needed to escape from her thoughts for a while. Usually it was frustration with either her father or Stephen that caused this need for escape, but this evening she just didn't want to dwell on that meeting at lunchtime.

'I'm entitled to holiday time, just like the rest of Atherton Publishing employees,' she dismissed with a shrug. 'So I took the afternoon off.' She just hadn't felt up to going back to the office, to face Stephen's curiosity about Robert Merlin, or a probable confrontation with her father.

So, after leaving Robert, she had sat forward in the taxi and told the driver she had changed her destination, giving him her home address instead. She'd spent most of the afternoon sitting in the bath, unreachable either personally or by telephone.

But she had heard her father arrive home ten minutes ago, heard him in his study as he poured himself a drink, so his arrival in the dining-room wasn't unexpected.

Her father glowered across at her. 'I'm not talking about your unexpected afternoon off, and you know it,' he bit out angrily.

She met his gaze steadily, her blue gaze calm. She had thought in the bath about what her reaction was going to be to this attack when it arrived, and had decided, if it came to it, that she was prepared to offer her resignation. In fact, to do so would solve a lot of her problems!

'Do I?' she returned coolly.

Her father began to pace the room, obviously furious. 'What did you think you were doing?' he finally exploded again. 'A change of editor for any author is a company decision, not a personal one.'

Arabella raised her brows. 'Unless that decision happens to have been made by you,' she derided.

'Possibly—yes!' He nodded decisively. 'I can't have my editors making those sorts of decisions without consulting me. Not even when that editor happens to be my own daughter! I felt a damn fool at lunch-time when Merlin explained exactly why the two of you were having lunch together.' He scowled.

Ah, now they were getting to the real heart of the

problem. A week ago her father had thought Merlin above himself as an author, but at the same time he had no intention of letting any employee—not even his own daughter!—use her initiative when it came to dealing with that author.

'I genuinely believe it is in Merlin's best interests if I don't continue to edit him.' And in her own, of course. Her emotions had been in a turmoil from the moment she'd first met the man! 'We agreed weeks ago that it's time Stephen started using all that education you paid for.' She quoted back at him easily one of the many complaints he had levelled at her brother since he left university.

There was an angry flush on her father's cheeks. 'Not as Merlin's editor,' he snapped coldly.

Arabella gave a dismissive shrug. 'I'm sorry, I thought that was what you had in mind when you sent Stephen to Merlin's home instead of me. I was just trying to make things easy for everyone,' she added innocently as she saw her father's guilty look at her reminder of what he had done the previous week.

Her father's eyes narrowed as he looked at her thoughtfully. 'You've changed, Arabella,' he said slowly.

She sat back in her chair. 'And I didn't think you had noticed,' she mocked softly.

'I'm not talking about discarding your glasses or having your hair cut,' he dismissed impatiently. 'Although why you had to have your hair cut I have no idea; your mother always liked it long.' He frowned.

Yes, she had. Arabella remembered that, at bedtime, her mother used to brush her hair for her until it shone, at the same time asking Arabella about her day. It had always been a special time that Arabella loved...

'Maybe when I was younger it wasn't as wild as it is now,' she conceded huskily. 'But Mummy has been gone a long time now; things change, situations change.' The subject had turned to her mother so naturally; she couldn't have asked for an easier opening if she had tried.

Her father returned her gaze uncomfortably. 'What do you mean?' he rasped defensively.

Arabella shrugged, all the time watching him closely. 'I'm just trying to say that Stephen and I are no longer children, that time has moved on. That people move on,' she added softly.

She had done a lot of thinking as she'd lain in the bath earlier. And not just about Merlin...

'Alison Wilder seems very nice,' she added lightly, at the lack of response from her father.

'She is!' That flush was back in his cheeks, but it didn't look like anger this time.

'What does she do?' Arabella was determined to continue the conversation.

'She edits a monthly fashion magazine,' he supplied tightly.

That gave an explanation of how the two of them could have met; it also explained how chic Alison had looked. The two certainly had publishing in common.

Arabella nodded. 'Perhaps you would like to invite her here for dinner one evening?'

His mouth tightened. 'Arabella—'

'Only if you want to, of course,' she encouraged casually, deliberately not meeting his gaze now. She was right about the seriousness of his relationship with Alison; she was sure she was.

'Of course I want to,' he snapped. 'I was going to discuss all of this with you at lunch today, if Merlin hadn't put me in that damned awkward position.' He scowled darkly. 'You—'

'Hello—anyone at home?' Stephen greeted them jovially from outside in the hallway. 'I hope so—because I've brought a guest home for dinner!'

Arabella was almost afraid to look up, had detected a note of panic in her brother's overly jolly voice. As far as she was aware, only one person had that particular effect on her brother...

She raised her head slowly as the door opened, and found herself looking straight at Robert Merlin.

'Good God, man!' Her father was the one to greet him in astonishment. 'After being a relative recluse for years you suddenly seem to be popping up all over the place!'

'I hope I'm not intruding,' Robert returned smoothly, but it was to Arabella he looked.

As far as she was concerned, this man always intruded. And, at the moment, doubly so.

He had interrupted a very private conversation between her father and herself. She had spent a lot of time thinking about her father's behaviour today, his unusual gesture in inviting her out to lunch, just the two of them, and then the way he'd had no trouble arranging to go with Alison Wilder instead of her, and the close intimacy between the couple.

She had come up with only one conclusion: her father was serious about the woman. That would also explain why he had previously been so secretive about her: she was too important for him to discuss lightly. He might even be thinking of marrying Alison!

After her initial surprise at the realisation, Arabella

had thought long and hard as to how she actually felt about this possibility. She'd meant exactly what she had said to her father minutes ago; her mother had been dead a long time now and it was time to move on, for all of them. If, in her father's case, that meant with Alison Wilder, then she was happy for both of them.

Quite where that left her as regarded continuing to live in this house, she wasn't absolutely sure. But she did know it was impossible to have two mistresses of one house. The thought of finally branching out on her own made her a little nervous, but at the same time it felt right. She felt exactly the same as she had over the question of having her hair cut: it was time.

'Not at all.' Again her father was the one to speak to him. 'Nice to see you again,' he added sociably.

Arabella had a feeling that, for all that he had intended talking to her at lunch today, her father was a little relieved at this interruption to their conversation. Even if that interruption had once again been made by Robert Merlin. And what did Stephen mean—dinner guest?

'I forgot to take this to Arabella at lunchtime, so I called in at the office this evening, only for Stephen to invite me to join you all for dinner,' Robert answered her father.

'This' turned out to be a large brown padded envelope which, until that moment, had remained unnoticed in his hand.

It was an all too familiar-looking envelope as far as Arabella was concerned, one she recognised very easily!

Since her visit to him last week, he must have finished the last Palfrey manuscript. But she had *no* intention of reading it.

She nodded, her expression coldly remote. 'Dinner is an excellent idea; it will give you and Stephen a chance to become better acquainted. Now, if you will all excuse me...' She didn't wait for a reply from any of them, walking determinedly towards the doorway.

Unfortunately she had to pass close by Robert to get there. His free hand came out to grasp her wrist. 'It's you I wanted to talk to,' he told her gruffly.

Arabella fixed her gaze on a point somewhere over his left shoulder; that one brief glimpse of him when he'd arrived, devastatingly handsome in dark suit and snowy white shirt, had been enough to set her pulse racing. A fact, she realised with an inward groan, he must be well aware of as his fingers lightly encircled her wrist!

'Stephen is your editor now,' she said flatly, twisting her arm out of his grasp, although her skin still tingled where he had held her. 'And I have a date this evening.' Now she did look up at him, stubbornly keeping her gaze level with his. Because she was lying about her previous engagement! But she had to get away.

His eyes had narrowed to icy slits. 'And not with your father this time,' he realised pointedly.

Her mouth twisted scathingly. 'Obviously not,' she acknowledged dryly.

'The man who is "no one serious"?'

Arabella gave a dismissive laugh. 'Not all of Emma's "feelings" are correct,' she told him enigmatically. 'Have a pleasant evening; I'm sure my father and Stephen will make you most welcome.' She turned towards the open doorway once again.

'Arabella!'

Her father sounded frustratedly angry. Which
wasn't surprising, she acknowledged wryly; he probably wanted to tell her exactly what he thought about
her dinner engagement, but was very much aware of
their guest.

She faced him with one brow raised questioningly.
'Yes?'

His eyes flashed with anger that he conveyed easily
to her. But again she could see he was very much
aware of Robert, the stranger in their midst. Martin
Atherton might usually be arrogantly bombastic, but
even he baulked at berating one of his children for
her lack of manners in front of a third party. It was
what she had counted on!

She was well aware of just how rude she was being;
even Stephen looked slightly taken aback at her behaviour—and was obviously more than a little ruffled
himself after having already spent a considerable
amount of time in this man's company. Arabella could
only inwardly sympathise with him—because she had
no intention of staying here and bearing the brunt of
Robert Merlin's sarcasm!

No doubt she would hear more on her behaviour
from her father later this evening or tomorrow, but,
for the moment, she didn't care; she did not want to
spend any more time in Robert Merlin's company today.

Because she had known earlier, when he'd kissed
her outside the restaurant, that it was the author she
was in love with, and not Palfrey. No matter what
game Robert chose to play with her emotions, she
knew it was just that: a game. Robert was as far out
of reach to her as the moon and the stars.

But he was obviously a man who disliked intensely being thwarted, used any means at his disposal—in this case her emotional weakness where he was concerned—to get his own way. He was determined she would remain his editor.

As determined as she was that she wouldn't! A case of 'the irresistible force meeting the immovable object'. An explosion, of sorts, was likely to follow. Which was why she was going out. Anywhere. As long as it was away from Robert.

'When will you be back?' her father asked tightly, the fierceness of his gaze still transmitting his anger.

She shrugged dismissively. 'I have no idea. Probably some time later this evening. I'll tell Mrs Willis on my way out that you have a guest for dinner.' Once again she turned to leave.

'Arabella...'

She halted in her tracks, her name having been spoken in not much more than a whisper this time—but it was Robert who had uttered it.

What did he want? What else was there to say? He seemed to think there was something...

She turned more slowly this time, steeling herself for this second confrontation. 'Yes?' she responded hesitantly, knowing her resolve was going to crumble if she didn't get out of here soon.

Robert looked at her without speaking for several long, long seconds, giving every appearance of being perfectly relaxed as he did so.

Arabella felt her tension rising, her hands clasped so tightly into fists, her nails were digging into her palms.

Then, very slowly, he smiled, a genuinely warm

smile that totally took her breath away. As did his next comment. 'Have a nice evening,' he said huskily.

Her legs almost gave way beneath her at the relief she felt that he hadn't said something controversial. 'Thank you,' she returned, suddenly finding she was blinking back tears. She wasn't going to cry! That would be her final humiliation!

She turned blindly back to the doorway, relieved when she managed to stumble through it this time, closing the door firmly behind her. She resisted the temptation to lean weakly back against it and, following the impetus, paused only long enough to pick up her handbag and car keys from the hallway table, and tell their housekeeper of the guest for dinner, before leaving the house as if she were being pursued.

In some ways she felt as if she was; Robert had been to her office, her favourite restaurant, and now to her home. She didn't feel she had anywhere she could go now where she wouldn't be reminded of him.

There was still Malcolm, she thought desperately as she drove her car out onto the road. He had wanted to see her this evening, but she had put him off. He had been more eager the last few days, possibly sensing the changes in her weren't only on the surface, and had telephoned her several times a day, when he had never really bothered before. He had even telephoned her this morning to see if she had changed her mind about going out with him this evening. She had said no at the time, but wasn't it a woman's prerogative to change her mind?

She changed direction at the next set of traffic lights, knowing where she was going now. She needed to be somewhere she felt wanted, with some-

one she didn't constantly have to be on her guard
against. She could forget all about Robert Merlin
when she was with Malcolm.

His car was on the forecourt as she drove in,
breathing a sigh of relief that he hadn't made other
plans for the evening after she'd turned him down.
Maybe it was even time she let their relationship develop into something a little deeper, gave in to his
repeated urgings to put their relationship on a physical
level.

Maybe it would be for all the wrong reasons—but
at this moment in time she didn't care!

She locked her car and quickly entered the building,
taking the lift up to Malcolm's apartment before she
lost her nerve. She could do this. Whoever heard of
a twenty-seven-year-old virgin anyway?

It seemed like for ever before she heard Malcolm's
movements inside the apartment in response to her
ring of the doorbell, although she was sure it was
really only a matter of a few minutes. It was her own
self-consciousness that was making her feel this way.
Which was silly. It was only Malcolm, for goodness'
sake. Only Malcolm? She had decided a few minutes
ago that he was to be her first lover!

She felt even more awkward when the door opened
a few seconds later and she saw Malcolm was in the
middle of dressing, probably to go out, his blond hair
still tousled from the shower, his shirt only partially
buttoned.

'Arabella...!' He seemed taken aback to see she
was his visitor. Malcolm was in his late forties, his
hair showing no signs of grey, his face pleasantly attractive rather than handsome, his eyes brown; he was
also very slim and fit for his age, the latter due for

the main part, Arabella knew, to regular visits to the gym.

His surprise at seeing her wasn't unexpected; she had never arrived at his apartment completely out of the blue like this before!

She gave him an over-bright smile. 'I wondered if I could change my mind about dinner?'

'I—Well—Of course,' he answered in a flustered voice. 'When did you have in mind?'

As Arabella knew only too well, he was a man of habit, always did the same thing at the same time every day of the week. And yet, Arabella thought with affectionate amusement, if she were to tell him he was a man who lacked spontaneity, he would vehemently deny it.

Perhaps this wasn't going to be all that difficult—after all, until a week ago she had been rather fond of him. Until Robert—No! She wouldn't think of him now. She wouldn't!

'Tonight,' she told him huskily, wondering how much longer he was going to keep her standing on the doorstep.

'Tonight...?' he echoed a little breathlessly. 'But I—I thought you were busy this evening?' He frowned.

'I changed my plans so that I could have dinner with you.' She smiled encouragingly.

'Well, I—That's marvellous!'

If it was so 'marvellous', why didn't he invite her into his apartment? Arabella thought impatiently.

'Malcolm, darling, will you be much longer?' a female voice called from inside. 'Only I really do have to go soon, and we—Oh, my God!' the woman groaned as she came into view behind Malcolm. 'You were so quiet out here, I thought whoever was at the door had gone...'

If the woman was surprised to see Arabella—and she undoubtedly was—then Arabella was even more surprised to see her!

She had suspected, even though he had never said so, that Malcolm had other female 'interests' in his life. But she knew this woman, recognised her all too easily from her occasional visits to the bank where Malcolm was manager. She was Malcolm's secretary. His married secretary!

She was dressed in what appeared to be a man's bathrobe, the overlong sleeves turned back, the belt tied tightly about the slenderness of her waist to keep the excess material from gaping.

In that split second Arabella realised Malcolm hadn't been in the process of dressing when she'd arrived, but undressing. Before joining his secretary in bed!

'Working late, Suzanne?' she somehow managed to enquire lightly, knowing that for pride's sake she had to bluff this out. To think that she had been planning to go to bed with this man herself. Now she realised she would have had to get in line. How humiliating!

The other woman still looked stricken, and Malcolm was the one to answer her. 'I can explain this, Arabella—'

'I'm sure you can,' she acknowledged pleasantly. 'But I think it would be better for all concerned if you didn't! Don't look so worried, Malcolm,' she added teasingly. 'There was never anything serious between the two of us, and your private life is your own business. And Suzanne's husband's, I suppose.' She frowned. How awful for the poor man; he probably did think his wife was working late at the office!

'You wouldn't tell him?' Suzanne had found her voice at last, her expression one of pure panic.

Arabella raised indignant brows. So much for dignity and pride! Her surprise for Malcolm had turned out to be much more of one for her. This was all very sordid. 'I have just told you that none of this is my business,' she said coldly. 'I suggest that you don't judge everyone else by your own lack of moral code,' she added bitingly before turning back to Malcolm. 'Please don't bother to call me again,' she told him evenly.

His dismay deepened. 'Arabella—'

'Goodbye, Malcolm,' she cut in firmly. 'Suzanne.' She nodded coolly to the other woman, before turning on her heel and walking away.

The shaking didn't start until she had made her descent in the lift, walked out to her car, unlocked it, and got inside. Then she couldn't seem to stop, her breath coming in ragged gasps.

How awful. How absolutely awful. She had never felt so humiliated in her life.

She had known there had to be at least one other 'someone' in Malcolm's life, and in truth it had never mattered to her in the past that there was. But to know was one thing; actually to be confronted with seeing the two of them together was something else entirely.

God, if she had arrived at Malcolm's apartment a few minutes later she might even have interrupted the couple in the middle of—No, she didn't even want to think about it!

Or about her own decision earlier to deepen her relationship with Malcolm!

Because if she had arrived *an hour* later the chances were she would have got into the bed still warm from his lovemaking with another woman.

Just the thought of it made her feel nauseous. So much so that she knew she had meant it when she'd told him she didn't want him to call her. She never wanted to see him again. She could never, ever trust a man who she knew had had an affair with another man's wife. If he cared so little for someone else's fidelity, how much did he value his own?

What was that saying? When one door closes, another door opens?

In her case it seemed to be that when one door closed another one slammed firmly shut in her face!

Malcolm's door, as far as she was concerned, would be very firmly closed in future.

CHAPTER EIGHT

'THE wanderer returns!'

Arabella gave a startled gasp at the sound of that voice, relaxing slightly when she realised it was Stephen who was talking to her.

'Wandering' just about described what she had been doing this evening. After leaving Malcolm's apartment so abruptly, she'd had no intention of returning home until she could be sure their unexpected dinner guest had left, so she had ended up driving around London for the last three hours!

She had discovered parts of London she'd never known existed before, despite having lived there all her life.

'It's all right, Arabella.' Stephen mocked her startled expression at having been caught trying to enter the house unnoticed—and failing miserably! 'Our dinner guest has gone,' he told her teasingly.

She instantly felt some of her tension leave her, although she knew her face remained pale.

Stephen frowned at her. 'Come through and share a brandy with me; you look as if you could do with one!'

A brandy would only put the warmth back into her chilled body; it couldn't restore her faith in men.

Any of them. Malcolm for his betrayal, her father for his arrogance, Stephen for his complacency, and Robert—well, of all of them she understood Robert the least. He was an enigma she couldn't even begin to work out. In fact, tonight she had decided to give up trying!

Stephen handed her a partly full brandy glass once they were in the drawing-room, still studying her closely. 'Not a successful evening.' He grimaced.

That had to be the understatement of the year. 'It certainly wasn't,' she acknowledged forcefully.

'I didn't mean yours,' her brother said impatiently, shaking his head. 'Your chap Merlin was—'

'He isn't mine,' she protested vehemently. And he never would be!

'Oh, but I'm afraid he is,' Stephen told her regretfully. 'As I was just about to explain, in contrast to the last time I met him, he was absolutely charming this evening. Very interesting to talk to. Apparently he lived in America for years. You know how interested I've always been in America,' he added eagerly.

Yes, she did. In fact, she wouldn't be surprised if her brother didn't end up living there himself one day. As for Robert having lived in America, she had realised that on seeing that photograph of Emma's mother.

But this wasn't the part of Stephen's conversation she was interested in... 'We seem to be deviating from the subject, Stephen,' she prompted tautly.

'What was—? Oh, yes.' He nodded as he recalled their original conversation. 'Well, it was a scintillating evening. I could see even Father found the chap interesting. But the upshot of it was,' he continued quickly as he could see Arabella's rising impatience with his waffling, 'that you're still Merlin's editor.'

'I'm not, you know,' she told him stubbornly, her gaze rebellious.

Stephen shrugged. 'I suggest you take that up with

Father. But in the meantime...' He produced that large brown padded envelope Merlin had delivered earlier in the evening, putting it on top of the coffee-table. 'Father asked me to give you this!'

Palfrey's last story!

Arabella stared at it as if it were a snake about to strike. 'Where is Father now?' She made no effort to pick up the envelope.

Stephen made a face. 'Gone off on one of his night-time jaunts.' He shrugged. 'I have no idea where, or with whom.'

But Arabella did: he was obviously with Alison Wilder. If her earlier hunch about the other woman was correct, it wouldn't be too far in the future before her father didn't disappear off for nights like this, but lived here with his new wife. Because Arabella had a feeling she and Stephen would very shortly be ac-quiring a stepmother...

She nodded. 'I'll talk to him tomorrow.' In the morning, if he bothered to return home before going to the office. Otherwise she would discuss it with him there; it was business, anyway.

Stephen frowned. 'I think you'll find there's noth-ing more to be said.'

Oh, yes, there was! And she was going to be the one saying it.

'What do you want me to do with this?' Stephen held up the bulky brown envelope.

She wanted him to throw it away. Destroy it. She wished it had never been written. She wanted him to take it and—

'Keep it clean, Arabella,' her brother warned as he easily read the war-like emotions in her expression.

She gave a weary sigh, taking a sip of her brandy,

feeling its warmth inside her before answering him. 'I suggest you take it—' she took another sip of her brandy '—and read it!' She smiled as Stephen looked relieved at the mildness of this answer instead of the more graphic one he had been expecting.

He looked at her consideringly. 'I don't know what it is about you, Arabella, but you seem different. And I don't mean in the way you look—although, I must say, you don't look half bad, sis.' He grinned at her appreciatively.

'Thank you, kind sir,' she accepted teasingly, sure that her cheeks were no longer pale, the brandy having given them warmth, along with the rest of her body.

'I can be kind,' he told her, disgruntled. 'I'm not always the spoilt brat, you know.'

'I do know, Stephen.' She smiled at him affectionately. 'And I'm not really different; I just seem to have reached a crossroads in my life. In all honesty, I don't know which way to go,' she added with a frown.

It was true—she didn't. She seemed to have reached an impasse with Robert and her father over this last Palfrey book, a situation where none of them would give an inch—Arabella because she just couldn't, and her father and Robert because it was just the nature of both men! But no one could make her do anything she didn't want to do. Although the alternative made her a little nervous... And a little excited, in an apprehensive sort of way. To leave this house, and Atherton Publishing, would be a very big step indeed.

But it might be one she had to take...

*   *   *

'Arabella?' Di spoke softly down the telephone receiver. 'That man is here to see you again.'

Arabella didn't need to ask this time who the man was. Di had that same awed tone to her voice as she had had the last time Robert Merlin had come to the offices. Arabella couldn't deny—inwardly—her own leap of emotions at the knowledge that he was downstairs; her pulse raced and her breathing became ragged.

But she had stubbornly kept to her decision concerning the last Palfrey book: Stephen had been the one to read the manuscript and send an acceptance letter to Robert Merlin—as if there had ever been any doubt about them publishing it! And Arabella had asked Stephen not to discuss it with her, had told him she wanted nothing to do with the novel or any future books by that particular author. Apart from going into raptures about how brilliant the book was—something else Arabella hadn't wanted to know!—Stephen had acceded to her request.

'Would you please inform Mr Merlin it's my brother he wishes to see and not me?' she told Di firmly.

There were several moments' silence on the telephone as Di obviously spoke to him, and then she came back on the line, sounding more flustered than ever. 'He insists it's you he wants to see!'

So that he could play games with her again? Arabella didn't think so. 'Would you please tell Mr Merlin I'm about to leave the office?' She made the sudden decision to have an early lunch, picking up her handbag and rising, ready to go. 'But I believe my brother is in his office.'

She knew damn well he was; Stephen was so

snowed under with work at the moment that he came
home every evening complaining he hadn't even had
time for a lunch break. Arabella sympathised with
him, but there was nothing she could do; she had
made her decision two weeks ago, and she intended
sticking to it. No matter what pressures were put on
her.

'I'll tell him, Arabella,' Di answered worriedly.
'But I don't think he's going to listen!'

Neither did Arabella, which was why she quickly
put down her phone, determined to make her escape
while she could. And escape it was. Robert had been
too quick for her last time, and she wasn't about to
let him repeat that victory.

Victory it would undoubtedly be. Because this had
turned into a war between them. It was almost like
one of Palfrey's campaigns. Except that Palfrey always won. And Arabella had no intention of Robert
doing so!

Except that before she could make good her escape
from her office a worried-looking Stephen burst in!
'My God, he's here again, Arabella!' Stephen had the
look of a hunted man. 'Do you think there was something wrong with the acceptance letter I sent him?'
He gave a concentrated frown. 'It was pretty straight-
forward, as I remember—'

'Stephen, I'm not interested,' she cut in firmly. 'I
told you and Father that weeks ago. Now I'm just on
my way out, so you'll have to deal with him yourself!'

'But what will I say? What—?'

'Well, for one thing, I would stop being afraid of
the man if I were you,' she told him impatiently. 'Otherwise—'

'Arabella's not frightened of me. Are you?' an all too familiar voice mocked from the open doorway.

All too familiar...

Once again, because of Stephen this time, she had failed to get away from this man.

She steeled herself to face the man she had so wanted to avoid, slowly turning to look at him, a bright, meaningless smile on her lips—a smile that almost slipped as she took in how breathlessly handsome he looked in a soft blue jumper and faded denims. The powder-blue colour of the sweater shouldn't have looked this good on him, but it only served to enhance the broadness of his shoulders and the blondness of his hair. Hair, she noticed inconsequentially that had been trimmed since she'd seen him two weeks ago...

She was suddenly angry with herself for even noticing that about him! The trouble was, she only had to close her eyes to know exactly what he looked like. It had been exactly the same two weeks since she'd last seen Malcolm, but she knew she would have difficulty visualising every feature of his face.

Not that Malcolm hadn't tried to see her again since that fateful evening at his apartment. He had telephoned her several times the next day, calls which she had refused to take. Then he had tried to see her at the office, but—unlike Robert Merlin—he had accepted her rejection through Di.

The telephone calls had continued in the following two weeks, but they were down to one a day now, and Arabella had cynically consoled herself that the only reason Malcolm was being so persistent was out of concern that she might tell someone of his affair with his married secretary. As if she were likely to do that! It was humiliating enough that she knew of her stupidity; she didn't have to tell the whole world about it!

At this moment she didn't have to close her eyes to see Robert either—he was standing right here in the room with her!

'Not in the least.' She answered his jibe easily, although her hands gripped her handbag a little tighter so that he wouldn't see their slight tremble. 'How are you, Merlin?' She deliberately used his professional name.

A fact he was well aware of as his mouth tightened slightly. 'Well, my editor refuses to talk to me, hasn't—apparently—even read my last manuscript, and, to add insult to injury, I receive a letter from her brother accepting my book! How do you expect me to be?' he concluded with cold challenge.

Stephen looked very unhappy at this attack. But Arabella refused to be disconcerted. Mainly because she knew that was what she and her brother were meant to be!

'You're being very stubborn about this, Merlin—'

'My name is Robert,' he ground out coldly. 'As for stubborn—would you mind leaving us, Atherton?' he requested harshly of Stephen. 'I think this conversation is private, between Arabella and myself,' he added arrogantly.

Stephen looked even more unhappy, although he was incapable of argument. This man was as arrogant as their own father, the difference being that Robert was their major author, and arguing with him would not endear any of them to their father. Arabella was past caring, but she knew that her brother wasn't.

'It's all right,' she told her brother scathingly. 'Perhaps it would be better if you didn't get involved in this conversation.' At least then, if it came to a crunch with their father afterwards, Stephen would be able to claim he took no part in it.

Stephen looked relieved at this chance to escape—although he was obviously concerned for Arabella too. 'You're sure you'll be all right?' He actually hesitated about leaving her alone with the other man.

'Didn't she just tell you she isn't afraid of me?' Robert cut in mockingly, moving to sit in the chair that faced Arabella's desk.

Stephen gave the other man a fleeting glance, his mouth tight. 'Yes. But—'

'I'll be fine, Stephen.' Arabella touched his arm reassuringly. 'You go off and have an early lunch. You've been working so hard recently, you deserve one!' She gave him an affectionate smile. 'Have a drink for me,' she added ruefully.

Her brother didn't need any further encouragement, hurrying from the office before thoughts of his work-load—or their father—could stop him. Arabella couldn't help but sympathise with him; their father had really turned the heat up over the last two weeks, putting pressure on him that Arabella was afraid might cause him to buckle.

She knew why her father was doing it, of course; he was really applying the pressure to her, knowing how fond she was of the younger brother she had helped to bring up. Their father had made all the other moves on her directly to bring her back into line, and when none of them had succeeded he had turned his attention on Stephen, in an effort to get to her that way.

But there was limited time left before even that

would become ineffective, and Arabella was optimistic that all this would stop. There would surely be no point to it then. She hoped so, for Stephen's sake.

'Do you feel in need of one?' Robert brought her attention back to him. 'A drink,' he explained at her puzzled expression.

She gave him a scathing glance, moving to stand behind her desk. 'Not in the least,' she dismissed easily. 'Why do you insist on being so difficult?' She frowned. For a man she had never met during the last five years of their working together, he was turning out to be their number one headache!

His eyes were narrowed. 'We've worked in relative harmony in the past; why change that?'

Until three weeks ago she had never met him; *that* had been when the trouble had begun!

She gave a weary sigh. 'Because—'

'You don't like the last Palfrey manuscript,' he finished harshly. 'You haven't even read the damned thing!' He stood up so forcefully that the chair moved back across the carpet, causing Arabella to recoil backwards. 'Don't worry, Arabella,' he bit out coldly. 'I've never struck a woman in my life. Intense though the provocation might have been!' he added grimly.

'I haven't provoked you—'

'You've provoked me in every damn way there is to provoke a man,' he cut in savagely, his hands clenched into fists at his sides, a nerve pulsing in his cheek. 'From the moment we first met—'

'You were extremely rude to me,' she interrupted accusingly, standing up herself now. 'I expected you to set your dogs on me at any moment!'

'Daisy and May wouldn't hurt a fly!' he dismissed scornfully.

'Unless you ordered them to!' she returned heatedly, tall and slender in fitted navy blouse and trousers.

He crossed the room so that he was standing only inches away from her, bending slightly so that their noses almost touched. 'Which I probably should have done,' he bit out. 'At least they would have kept you in one place long enough for me to talk some sense into you!' He scowled at her.

Arabella glared right back. 'You're the one who refuses to see sense!' Her voice rose slightly in her agitation. 'You're committing professional suicide—and you refuse to listen to anyone brave enough to tell you that!'

His mouth twisted. 'Meaning you?'

'Meaning me!' she confirmed forcefully, breathing hard in her anger.

'You aren't being brave, Arabella,' he snapped viciously. 'The opposite, if anything!'

Her eyes widened furiously at his implication. 'Having met you, I no longer wish to work with you,' she conceded scathingly. 'But that's only because I find you arrogant, pigheaded, uncooperative in the extreme—'

'You could almost be talking about yourself,' he challenged harshly.

She drew in a sharp breath. 'Only "almost"?'

He shrugged, his eyes still glacial. 'You aren't always uncooperative,' he bit out coldly.

She knew exactly what he meant, knew he had to be referring to the times she had been in his arms, when her response to him had been so obvious! 'That was before I realised exactly what an arrogant bast—'

'Having another lovers' tiff?' mocked a voice from

the doorway. 'Really, Arabella, Merlin,' her father continued lightly as he came into the room and closed the door firmly behind him, 'couldn't you find somewhere a little less public for these verbal displays of passion the two of you seem to so enjoy engaging in? This office certainly isn't the place, where everyone can hear you, and anyone can just walk in on you.'

Arabella had been outraged at his opening comment about a 'lovers' tiff,' but as he continued in that same teasing vein she felt like actually hitting him. What on earth did he think he was implying?

'If you were somewhere more private you could have kissed her until she was senseless by now,' he told Robert pleasantly. 'That would have settled this argument once and for all.'

'Really, Father!' Arabella gasped her outrage. 'Just because you have decided you and Alison are deeply in love, that is no reason to suppose everyone else around you feels the same way. Robert and I hate each other!'

'Don't be ridiculous, Arabella,' her father dismissed, as if chiding a child. 'The air fairly crackles with emotion when the two of you are in the same room together.'

'I just told you, with hate!' she burst out defensively. Why didn't Robert say something, tell her father how ridiculous he was being, instead of just standing there listening?

'I'm dreadfully sorry about this, Robert.' Her father turned to him. 'But it seems that certain parts of my daughter's education have been neglected. It's because her mother died when she was so young, of course.' He frowned. 'But, nevertheless, I should have done something to rectify that omission. Of course,

now that Alison and I are to be married, Arabella will
have a stepmother she can talk to. Although I think
it's possibly been left a little too late.' He grimaced
apologetically. 'Sorry about that, Robert,' he said
again.

Arabella was growing angrier and angrier as her
father continued speaking; anyone would think she
wasn't even here, and was incapable of speaking up
for herself! Which she most certainly wasn't. She
wouldn't have done it in the way her father was doing; he sounded as if he was apologising for a rebellious child!

'I had no idea congratulations were in order.'
Robert frowned, holding out his hand to the other
man. 'Arabella didn't mention it.' He looked at her in
what, to Arabella, seemed an accusing way.

There had hardly been an opportunity for her to
indulge in any social pleasantries; they had been too
busy arguing!

'When is the wedding?' Robert prompted Martin
Atherton interestedly.

'Two weeks' time. I know, I know.' Her father
laughed self-consciously as the younger man looked
surprised at the speed with which things were pro-
gressing. 'But, having met Alison yourself, I'm sure
you can understand why I'm rushing her into marriage,' he added pointedly.

'I can indeed,' Robert acknowledged dryly. 'She's
a very beautiful woman. You're a very lucky man.'

Well, obviously Robert would think that; he had
found Alison attractive himself!

'I think so.' Her father nodded, looking happier
now than Arabella had ever seen him before.

Having met Alison several times herself now,

Arabella could understand why. As well as being beautiful, the other woman was really warm and friendly, taking great pains where Arabella was concerned not to appear like an intruder. But Alison needn't really have worried on that score; Arabella liked her very much, and thought her father lucky to have found someone so lovely.

'You'll come to the wedding, of course, Merlin?' her father invited effusively. 'Alison would be so pleased if you did. She was mortified after you left the restaurant that day, because she hadn't instantly recognised you. She's one of your biggest fans.' He beamed. 'Reads all of your books.'

Robert gave a gracious nod in acceptance of the compliment. 'It's as well that someone does,' he returned softly, the jibe obviously meant for Arabella as he looked at her challengingly.

'Bring your lovely young daughter too,' her father continued unconcernedly. 'The two of you can accompany Arabella. She—'

'Have you quite finished?' Arabella cut in furiously, having found her voice at last. She didn't believe them! It was bad enough that they seemed to be discussing her as if she weren't there, but she drew the line at her father actually arranging for Robert and Emma to be with her at the wedding! 'I can arrange my own partner, if you don't mind!' she told her father indignantly. He wouldn't be Robert Merlin, and he wouldn't be Malcolm, either…she added silently.

'Well, you don't seem to be seeing that chap Malcolm any more.' Her father read her thoughts. 'It's a pity that you and Robert will be there on your own—'

'Leave it for now, Martin,' Robert cut in smoothly

as he could obviously see Arabella was about to explode again. 'We'll work something out,' he added confidently.

If, by that, he meant he would talk her into accompanying him to the wedding, then he was in for a surprise!

'I hope so.' Her father nodded happily, obviously extremely content in his relationship with Alison. 'Perhaps the two of you ought to take a leaf out of our book and get married; you argue enough to be husband and wife already!'

Arabella watched wordlessly as the men shared an amused laugh—at her expense! She didn't believe her father had just said what he had. She and Robert get married? There was more likelihood of her becoming the second female Prime Minister of England than there was of her marrying this man—and she had no aspirations to the former at all!

'Well, I'll leave the two of you to—settle this.' Her father moved to the door. 'In any case, I'll see you at the wedding in two weeks' time, Merlin.' He glanced at Arabella, noting the glaring anger in her eyes, the two bright spots of colour in her cheeks, and turned back to the other man with a grimace. 'I'll get Alison to send you a separate invitation. Just in case,' he added by way of parting.

Arabella just stared at the closed office door once her father had gone. She still couldn't believe he had said those things! She knew he was in love, was wildly happy with Alison, but really—!

'I think, before you explode,' Robert said softly from very close behind her, 'that I'll just take your father's advice.'

She stared at him uncomprehendingly. Which part

of her father's advice? He had been so full of it! What—?

Robert's arms moved about her and pulled her close to him. 'I think he was right about my kissing you until you're senseless!'

That part of the advice, Arabella had time to note, before Robert's mouth came down forcefully on hers and she found herself crushed against the hardness of his body.

It was as if she had been waiting for this since the moment she'd seen him again, her body seeming to melt into his, her lips returning the pressure of his, parting to allow full access to his marauding tongue.

One of his hands caressed the deep red tendrils of hair at her nape, sending shivers of delight down the entire length of her spine, his other hand cupping one side of her chin now as he held her face up so that he could sip at and taste her lips at his leisure, finally raising his head slightly to look down at her with challenging eyes. 'You are the stubbornest woman I've ever met in my life,' he murmured as he stroked her hair back from her burning cheeks.

'Mmm,' she agreed dazedly, just wanting him to kiss her again.

She wanted him so much, her whole body was alive and tingling with the emotion. She needed him to make love to her.

He gave a relaxed laugh, pulling her down with him as he sat in the leather chair that faced her desk, settling her comfortably on his knee. 'Careful, Arabella,' he murmured huskily. 'We just agreed on something again. We could make a habit of it!'

Arabella wished he would stop talking and just kiss her again. And then he did—and it was deeper and stronger than ever before, both of them hungry for the passion that flared between them, hands searching, caressing, becoming fevered in their need, so that Arabella lost all sense of time and place, of everything but the searing pleasure of Robert's hands as he gently caressed her breasts beneath her silky blouse.

She gasped out loud as those marauding fingers touched her already hardened nipples, pleasure unlike anything else she had ever known coursing through her body to her thighs, and she felt the rush of warmth there, the beginning of an ache she didn't even know how to start to assuage.

But Robert did, pushing aside her blouse so that his lips might close moistly over a nipple through the silky material, the erotic touch of his tongue against her skin through the gossamer material making her groan low in her throat. Robert's hands were against her thighs now, which parted for him like petals in the spring.

'Oh, God, Arabella,' Robert groaned, his forehead damp against hers. 'Your father was right about something else; I can't kiss you here!' he explained hoarsely as Arabella looked at him with wild, dazed eyes. 'Anyone could walk in. We need to go somewhere else, somewhere where I can make love to you until we're both too weak to do anything else but fall asleep in each other's arms!'

She was still flushed with pleasure, his words only slowly sinking in past the storm of passion that had threatened to engulf her. Had threatened? Why was she already thinking in the past tense?

Because that mind-numbing passion was fading, and with it came the return of clear thinking. What was she doing? More to the point, look at who she was doing it with!

'We can't go to your home, Arabella.' He shook his head, his forehead still resting against hers, the warmth of his breath stirring the hair at her temple. 'I only came here for the day this time so I haven't booked into a hotel. But that doesn't mean we—'

'Stop right there!' Arabella cut in harshly, struggling up out of his arms, pushing away from him, needing to put some distance between them, meeting no opposition as Robert was the one to look dazed now.

It took her several long seconds to refasten her blouse, much longer than it had taken Robert to unfasten it! The realisation just made her angry all over again, this time more at herself than at him. He couldn't be blamed for coming to the conclusion that he had, not when she had obviously been so willing.

She shook her head, standing up now. 'I'm not about to book into a hotel or anywhere else with you!' she told him vehemently.

He briefly closed his eyes, running weary fingers over his frowning forehead before looking at her again. 'I've done this all wrong again somehow,' he sighed raggedly. 'It's as I said to Emma at lunch that day; I'm out of practice at this sort of thing.'

And she knew exactly the reason for that; he had never got over his broken marriage...

'Well, you aren't going to get back into practice with me!' Arabella glared at him.

'Arabella—'

'As you've just said, you didn't intend staying in London this time, and you've said what you came here to say, so now I suggest you leave!' She stood across the room from him, putting as much distance between them as she could in the confines of the office, her breasts quickly rising and falling in her agitation. Breasts that only minutes ago Robert had touched, kissed—She had to stop this! 'Right now,' she added coldly.

He no longer looked dazed, sitting forward in the chair. 'I'll go when I'm good and ready,' he rasped harshly, his eyes a glacial blue. 'I don't know what's the matter with you, warm and passionate one minute, the next cold as ice, but if that's the way you want to be, then so be it.' He stood up abruptly, his gaze becoming contemptuous as she took an involuntary step backwards. 'Don't worry, Arabella, I've never had to force myself on a woman in my life!'

Of course he hadn't; he hadn't needed to with a wife as beautiful as the actress Kate Lawrence! For here was the root of her fear of this man. He had been married to a woman who was openly acclaimed as one of the most beautiful in the world. A woman who, a few years ago, had been kidnapped and held to ransom.

The story had been in the newspapers for days: Robert Lawrence's distress, his attempts to raise the money the kidnappers were demanding, the fact that his father-in-law was finally the one to come up with the money and secure his daughter's release.

But the kidnapping had changed the lives of the main characters for ever, it seemed, because Kate Lawrence hadn't been able to forgive her husband for not providing the ransom money, the two of them divorcing only months later, the actress brokenhearted and tearful, Robert Lawrence stony-faced and close-mouthed.

The tragedy had happened six years ago. Robert Lawrence, a scriptwriter highly acclaimed in his own right, had left Hollywood when, almost immediately after the divorce, his ex-wife had married the man who had been comforting her since her harrowing ordeal. He had taken his young daughter Emma with him, apparently never to be heard of again.

But Arabella knew who he was, where he was, knew now why he would only ever have his books published under the name of Merlin; he didn't want anyone to know exactly who he was and have that old heartache resurrected.

Arabella knew, with a certainty that was heartbreaking in itself, that it was madness to fall in love with a man who had loved his wife so deeply, he felt he could never trust a woman with his heart again...

CHAPTER NINE

'I'M NOT about to start now, with you,' Robert added with hard dismissal. 'Stephen has a copy of the last Palfrey manuscript.' He walked over to the door. 'Read it or not, I don't give a damn any more!'

One minute he was there, all-pervasive, the next he was gone, closing the door behind him with barely controlled violence. As soon as that door shut, Arabella became aware of the hot tears coursing down her cheeks.

She wanted to run after him, stop him leaving, knew that if she didn't she would never see him again.

But if she did run after him, somehow managed to put things right between them, what then! A brief affair that, when it ended, as it surely would, would leave her as desolate and inconsolable as he had been when his wife had divorced him?

But she loved him. Loved him so much she ached with it. Although she was afraid of him too, knew that to be with him was to face the certainty of loving him and then losing him. Better not to love him at all.

And yet she did. Not Palfrey. Not some mythical hero. But Robert Merlin. Robert Merlin Lawrence.

She had to stop this, had to get her life back under control. She had made some serious decisions over the last two weeks; she would concentrate on them. Had to concentrate on them if she wanted to maintain her sanity!

But, first of all, she had her father and Alison's

wedding to get through. A wedding she was sure Robert wouldn't attend now. As he had said, he had no intention of forcing himself on anyone. She had made it more than clear that she wanted him to stay away from her.

No, Robert wouldn't be at her father's wedding...

Nevertheless, amongst all of the plans she had to put into practice during the following two weeks, she kept checking with Alison to see if Robert or Emma had replied to the invitation she knew had been sent out to them. Their silence wasn't exactly reassuring because even though there had been no acceptance there had been no refusal either.

Damn the man!

What game was he playing now? Cat and mouse—with her as the tormented mouse? It was no good telling herself she didn't care whether he was there or not. Because she did care, very much. But, at the same time, there was no way she couldn't be at the wedding. The main reason for that wasn't her father, but Alison.

She had come to know the other woman quite well during the last few weeks, liked her very much, and knew that Alison was worried about usurping her place at the Atherton home. Arabella had taken great pains to convince her that, contrary to usurping her, she was freeing her!

Arabella was genuinely pleased at the couple's happiness, especially so for her father, having no doubt that he had at last found someone he loved and wanted to spend the rest of his life with. For Arabella not to attend the wedding now, not to act as Alison's attendant, after all that she had done over the last few weeks to reassure them of her genuine joy in their marriage, would only convince them that she had been putting on an act for their benefit.

And she hadn't. She truly hadn't. The advent of Alison into her father's life had given Arabella a freedom she hadn't even realised was missing from her life. Now she could live where she liked, work where she liked, and not have to feel she was letting anyone down by doing so. These were freedoms in themselves.   Which was why, on the day of the wedding, she was quite happy to fulfil her role as Alison's attendant. Alison's parents were both dead, her uncle intending to meet them at the church to give the bride away. So it had been agreed that Arabella's father would move out of the family home and into a hotel the night before the wedding, taking Stephen with him, leaving Alison to dress and leave from the Atherton home.

It had seemed the most sensible thing all round; Alison's things had already been moved into the master bedroom alongside her husband-to-be's, and the two of them were leaving on a two-week honeymoon later today before coming back to the Atherton house as husband and wife.

Alison made an absolutely beautiful bride. Never having been married before, she had wanted to wear a white wedding dress and veil, to do all the things that other first-time brides did, although usually they were much younger than her. She had waited for marriage until she'd found the right man, and Arabella was so glad it had turned out to be her father.

She had been slightly concerned at first, because she knew her father's real views on women having careers. But Alison, for all she was warm and kind, also had a very strong will; her career would continue.

Arabella's father had been dragged into the twentieth century at last!

It was because Arabella wanted the other woman to know how warmly she approved of the marriage that she had a special gift for her stepmother-to-be.

'Something old,' she told Alison warmly as she opened the jewellery box that lay in the palm of her other hand, revealing a gold Victorian necklace in the shape of a heart. 'It belonged to my grandmother,' she explained, at Alison's wide-eyed look. 'And my mother left it to me,' she added huskily, wanting Alison to know just how much she welcomed her into the family.

Alison looked alarmed. 'Oh, I couldn't!' she protested breathlessly, looking absolutely radiant in the flowing white satin gown, tiny white flowers adorning her hair beneath the veil.

'Please.' Arabella had half expected this protest. 'Daddy was only forty when Mother died,' she continued as she removed the necklace from the box. 'My mother knew she was dying. She never wanted him to remain alone, Alison.' She smiled encouragingly. 'Stephen and I are so pleased he waited for you.'

Alison's green eyes were moist with emotion. 'I am too,' she told her gruffly. 'And I'll gladly wear the necklace, Arabella.' She accepted the delicate gold chain being fastened about her slender neck. 'But as something borrowed,' she added gently. 'I think, if this was your mother's, that your father might like to see you wear it at your own wedding one day.'

Arabella smiled. 'He might like it—but it will never happen!'

Alison touched her cheek affectionately. 'Us career women are the ones that bite the dust the hardest, you know!' she said self-derisively, well aware of her fiancé's change of heart concerning women who worked. She knew how difficult it must have been for Arabella these past few years.

Arabella didn't protest at the label—although, in truth, she had always been far from that. If the right man for her had come along she would have given up her career without a qualm. Well, he had come along—and, just as quickly, had gone again! Now her career was all-important to her.

'Possibly,' she answered evasively. 'I think we had better get you to the church—before my father thinks you aren't coming at all and gets himself into even more of a state than when he left here last night!' Her usually self-confident father had begun to resemble a gibbering wreck as the wedding had got nearer!

Alison smiled at the thought of her fiancé. 'Yes, I—Oh, my goodness,' she groaned suddenly, looking stricken. 'I'm just as bad! It's been such a rush this morning, what with the florist arriving, the hairdresser, all the last-minute details for the caterers, that I completely forgot to tell you that your father rang—'

'He isn't supposed to talk to you before the wedding, either,' Arabella protested at this breach of protocol.

'But in the rush of leaving last night he forgot to tell us.' Alison was agitated, frowning worriedly. 'Robert Merlin rang him yesterday; he's going to be at the wedding!'

Arabella felt herself pale, knew that she must be almost as white as Alison's wedding gown. Robert was going to be at the wedding... He had left it until the last minute to let anyone know, but he was going to be there!

'I'm so sorry I forgot to tell you, Arabella.' Alison squeezed her hand. 'Apparently he's been away, and only got back home yesterday.'

When he had instantly rung up to accept the invitation. Why? What possible reason could he have for being there? Oh, he was one of Atherton Publishing's most prestigious authors, the biggest single money-earner, but why did Robert want to be at the wedding of a man he barely knew—and a woman he had met only once?

'Arabella, do you want me to try to contact your father?' Alison looked at her concernedly. 'He could—'

'No! No,' she repeated more calmly, inwardly berating herself for reacting in this way. So Robert was going to be at the wedding. So what? She was the daughter of the groom, attendant of the bride, and she had a role to play; she would have no time for anything other than socialising with all of the guests. Of which Robert was only one. 'It isn't important,' she dismissed easily, back in control again. 'And as for contacting my father, he should already be at the church!'

Alison looked at her wristwatch. 'Oh, goodness, yes. We had better go,' she agreed, hurrying to the bedroom door, and then coming to an abrupt halt, turning back uncertainly to Arabella. 'I—'

'You look beautiful,' Arabella assured her warmly as she joined her at the door. 'My father will think so. Everyone will think so. How could they possibly do anything else?' she teased, gently steering Alison in the direction of the stairs.

Alison gave a throaty laugh. 'It's too late to do anything about it now, anyway! You look lovely too,

Arabella. I'm so pleased you agreed to wear that dress.' She looked appreciatively at the peach satin dress Arabella wore.

'I always wanted to be a bridesmaid—but I had no idea I would be twenty-seven when it happened!' she said self-derisively. In her case it was going to be 'once a bridesmaid, never a bride'!

The drive to the church was over all too soon, everything seeming to happen as if in a dream once they arrived. Alison's uncle was there waiting for them, and the three of them walked down the aisle as the specially chosen music began to play.

The church was packed with family and friends, too many for Arabella to be able to put names to all the faces. Certainly too crowded for her to be able to pick out one particular person...

But he was here—she somehow sensed that he was—although once they reached the altar she made a point of keeping her gaze straight ahead, concentrating on the service. Her father and brother looked wonderful in their morning suits, the responses of the bride and groom made with quiet dignity.

It was only when it came time to walk back down the aisle, accompanied by her brother this time as they followed the bride and groom, that Arabella again allowed herself to look for Robert in the crowd. She still couldn't see him. But she knew that as she was one of the principal players in this wedding he must be able to see her, must be aware that she looked like something off the top of the Christmas tree in the peach gown and with cream flowers adorning her hair! But Alison had wanted a proper wedding, with an accompanying bridesmaid—and only Arabella knew how fitting that title was for her!

The photographs posed for outside the church seemed to take for ever, and it took every effort on Arabella's part to keep smiling. But she had no intention of letting anyone think she wasn't one hundred per cent happy with this marriage.

Several newspapers that had picked up on the story of the engagement and marriage of the head of Atherton Publishing had tried to imply as much over the last couple of weeks. As a family they had decided to ignore such fabrications. Because the truth of the matter was, this marriage couldn't have come at a better time for Arabella. It couldn't have worked out better if she had introduced the couple herself!

'You look beautiful, Arabella.'

Her smile wavered drastically at the sound of Robert's voice so close behind her. She had stepped back while photographs were taken of her father and Alison on their own.

She carefully arranged her features into a coolly welcoming smile before turning to face Robert. But, no matter how carefully she might have composed herself, she still wasn't prepared for how devastatingly attractive he looked in the dark suit and snowy white shirt. Or for the realisation of how much she still loved him!

Would it never go away? Was her love for him to be with her for the rest of her life?

'Arabella?' He frowned at her lack of response.

Speak, damn it, she inwardly instructed herself. She couldn't just continue to stand here staring at him like this. She had known he was here; now she had to deal with it.

She drew in a deeply controlling breath, forcing that smile back on her lips. 'I look like the fairy on top of the tree,' she contradicted him self-derisively. 'But it was what Alison wanted.' She shrugged dismissively. 'Where's Emma?' She looked about them curiously when she couldn't immediately see the young girl.

'Visiting her grandfather,' Robert supplied abruptly. 'I think they're ready to move now.' He nodded in the direction of the rest of the wedding party as they began to move towards the cars waiting to take them to the hotel where the reception was being held.

Somehow—and Arabella could never explain afterwards how it had happened—she ended up in the second car with Robert, Stephen somehow having been left behind!

'How have you been?' he prompted gruffly minutes later as their vehicle followed the car carrying the bride and groom.

In truth, she had been very well—as long as she kept away from thoughts of this man and concentrated on the job in hand. In fact, she had managed very well. Surprisingly so, when she sat back and looked at her achievements.

'Well, thank you,' she answered abruptly. 'You?' She frowned at him as she asked the question—because on closer inspection he looked rather grim, lines of strain beside his eyes and mouth. She didn't fool herself for a minute that this had anything to do with her. 'Emma is with her grandfather, you said?' Her frown deepened; there had never been any mention of a grandfather...

'Yes,' he confirmed tersely. 'Are your father and Alison going away after the wedding?'

End of the subject of Emma's visit to her grandfather. Arabella found she wasn't altogether happy with that; she sensed there was much more to this than Robert was telling her. But she also knew him well enough to realise that if he didn't want to tell her any more then he wouldn't!

'They are.' She nodded. 'Although I believe their destination is a secret,' she added indulgently—because she knew very well they were off to Bermuda; her father had told her. In confidence, of course.

That was the end of that subject too. At the rate they were going they would run out of things to say before they even reached the reception! Thank goodness it wasn't far to go to the hotel now. In her opinion she had performed her social role where this man was concerned; she could safely ignore him for the rest of the day.

Good grief, they were in a situation now where not only did they not agree on any subject raised, but they could find little to say on the ones they used to be able to talk about more freely! Arabella certainly wasn't going to broach the subject of his writing; she had made a point of not discussing it with Stephen, had no idea how that particular relationship was going, and, in the circumstances, she had no intention of talking to Robert about it either.

'The weather is nice for this time of year, isn't it?' Robert spoke softly at her side.

Arabella gave him a puzzled look. What—? Her brow cleared as she saw the laughter in his eyes and realised exactly what he was doing. 'As early summers go, yes.' She gave the appropriate answer; they hadn't really progressed very far since that day they'd had lunch together at Mario's! Although her own life had changed completely...

She gave a start of surprise as Robert reached over and took her hand into his, entwining his fingers with hers. She looked at their linked fingers, hers so much tinier than his, white and delicate; Robert's were tanned and strong. The touch of that hand had completely disconcerted her, thrown her resolve where this man was concerned into complete confusion.

He seemed different today, she realised as she looked at him from beneath lowered lashes. It wasn't just those lines beside his eyes and mouth. Then she realised what it was; he hadn't said one challenging or insulting word to her since he had spoken to her outside the church! Ridiculous, but somehow she found that even more unnerving…

'How are you really, Arabella?' he prompted gently, looking at her searchingly.

Just what did he mean by that? She had answered him truthfully the first time he'd asked. Things were going well, and—

'I would have telephoned you,' he continued gruffly when she didn't answer. 'But after the last time we—spoke I wasn't sure what my reception would be.'

Had she ever been pleased to see this man? Not since she had realised Merlin was Palfrey! Certainly not since she had realised she was in love with him. And not since she had discovered that his ex-wife was one of the most beautiful women in the world, an actress loved and admired by millions, a woman who, when she'd divorced him, had left him bitter and broken-hearted.

'I'm sure my father will appreciate the fact that you've made the effort to come to his wedding,' she answered evasively.

He frowned. 'And you, Arabella, are you pleased to see me here too?'

What was she supposed to answer to that? She certainly wasn't about to humiliate herself any further by saying yes. Besides, she wasn't sure if it was true. If she didn't see this man, didn't think about him, then the pain of loving him was just that little bit less...

His mouth tightened. 'I can tell by your expression you aren't,' he bit out tautly. 'Arabella, I—'

'Here we are,' she said brightly—thankfully!—as the car pulled up outside the hotel and the driver got out to open the door for them. 'I really do have to go inside, Robert,' she told him pointedly as he made no move to get out of the car. 'Obviously Stephen and I are the main attendants.' She had no idea where her brother was; he was the one who should have been in this car with her!

'Arabella, I need to talk to you.' Robert's fingers tightened about hers.

'Not here,' she told him agitatedly; she had nothing to say to him. 'And certainly not now,' she added impatiently, getting out of the car.

To her chagrin Robert got out beside her—still firmly holding her hand. As several other wedding cars had arrived at the same time they were attracting quite a lot of curiosity; she knew most of these people, and the majority knew she didn't have a steady relationship. Great! Now it wouldn't only be the Press that were watching her every move; now she would have to put up with everyone else's curiosity and speculation about her. As if things weren't difficult enough already!

'Arabella, what the hell were you—? Robert!' Stephen greeted warmly as he recognised the other man. 'Sorry, I didn't realise it was you.' He shook Robert's hand. 'All I saw was Arabella disappearing into the distance with some man—minus me!'

'My fault,' Robert claimed abruptly, obviously not happy about this interruption.

'No problem,' her brother dismissed easily. 'I cadged a lift with one of the other guests. Shall we rejoin the others?' He grimaced at the prospect, not at all comfortable with his own role in this wedding.

Arabella had hoped that Robert would take the hint at this point and rejoin the other guests, leaving Stephen and herself to carry out their official duties. But no such luck. He took a proprietorial hold of her arm and accompanied her and Stephen inside the prestigious hotel!

Her father and Alison were waiting at the door of the reception room to greet all their guests, the two of them looking ecstatically happy now that the wedding ceremony was over. Arabella wished she felt as comfortable; she had a feeling the difficult part had just begun for her!

'I think you're going to love the artwork on the new Palfrey cover.' Stephen spoke eagerly to the other man.

'I'm sure I will,' Robert accepted woodenly.

'We've really worked hard on it, and—'

'Stephen, this is not the time,' Arabella told him sharply as they approached her father and Alison.

Robert's mouth twisted. 'Your sister has washed her hands of the Palfrey books,' he reminded Stephen harshly.

She drew in an indignant gasp, two bright spots of colour on her cheeks. 'I—'

'Not only the Palfrey books,' Stephen answered the

other man. 'Arabella has washed her hands of the lot of us!'

'I have not!' she protested, looking sharply at Robert and noting his sudden, frowning interest. Of course he didn't know! How could he? The last time they had spoken it had hardly been conciliatory. Had it ever! 'It isn't like that, Stephen, and you know it,' she muttered awkwardly.

'What isn't like that?' Robert was still watching the two of them closely.

'Stephen, Aunt Catherine just came in,' Arabella told him quickly. 'And she's on her own. One of us should go over and make sure she sits with someone she can talk to.'

'One of us should,' Stephen agreed, following her line of vision to where their elderly great-aunt had just finished giving her good wishes to the bride and groom, a tall, autocratic woman dressed in her usual black, despite the happiness of the occasion. She had terrified the life out of Arabella and Stephen when they were children! 'But why does it have to be me?' Stephen muttered, showing he was still in awe of the old lady.

'Because you're her favourite great-nephew,' Arabella told him, firmly turning him in the direction of their great-aunt.

A move he resisted. 'I'm her only great-nephew!'

'Exactly,' Arabella acknowledged with satisfaction. 'She'll cut you out of her will if you don't dance attendance on her! It's too late for me,' she added quickly, as he was about to protest again. 'I disgraced myself in her eyes years ago by choosing to go out to work.' She was very much aware of Robert's close attention to their conversation, and wished her brother would just go!

'So you did.' Stephen grinned. 'I could be even more in her favour once I've told her about your latest escapade. Or do I mean lucky escape…?' he muttered as he moved off towards their aunt, leaving Arabella alone with Robert once more.

They might have been the only two people in the room, so tense was the atmosphere between them suddenly. In fact, Arabella was unable even to look at Robert, his tension tangible in the air that crackled between them.

He suddenly grasped both her arms, pulling her close against him as he turned her to face him. 'What did he mean, Arabella?' he ground out harshly, his expression grim.

'Let go of me, Robert,' she muttered forcefully. 'People are staring!' They were attracting more attention than the bride and groom at this particular moment.

A pulse was beating erratically in his clenched jaw. 'I don't give a damn what—'

'Robert!' her father greeted him loudly, smiling as he quickly crossed the room to where they stood together like two statues frozen in time. 'I'm glad you could make it after all.' The hand he held out to Robert forced him, out of necessity, to release his grip on one of Arabella's arms. The two men shook hands. But Robert only released that one arm; his grip was even tighter on Arabella's other one, as if he thought she might make her escape if it weren't.

As indeed she probably would have done. She didn't want to talk to him, had nothing left to say. But he obviously didn't share that view, both hands holding her tightly again now. Almost every time she saw this man she ended up with bruises on her skin. He really was the most—

'Martin, I want to know what's going on,' he told the other man grimly. 'Arabella, for once, appears to have little to say,' he added dryly.

Her father kept his smile on his face, the people around them returning to their own conversations again now. 'What appears to be the problem, Robert? What do you want to know?'

'Father—'

'It appears to be your silence that has created Robert's puzzlement in the first place; I suggest you let me answer his questions,' her father told her softly.

'But—'

'Arabella,' her father reproved softly. 'I can't have a guest upset at my wedding.'

'I'm upset,' she protested.

'But you aren't a guest,' he reasoned. 'Robert?' He turned back to the other man.

Arabella stared at the two incredulously. They couldn't do this to her. She didn't care if her father was trying to avoid a scene at his wedding; she was not going to be treated this way.

'Robert is upset because no one has informed him of things that happen to be none of his business!' she said sarcastically, her cheeks red with anger.

'Really?' Her father remained calm. 'What sort of things?' he prompted Robert.

'I believe I just said they were none of his business!' she snapped indignantly.

'I'm making them my business.' Robert's voice was controlled—too much so, his grip on her arm evidence of his continuing tension.

'What sort of things?' her father repeated mildly.

Robert drew in a ragged breath. 'Is Arabella still an employee of Atherton Publishing?'

'You—'

'As of yesterday, no.' Her father answered the other man as if Arabella hadn't tried to protest—yet again!

Robert turned to her with narrowed eyes. 'Did you resign or were you pushed out?'

'I resigned, of course,' she gasped defensively. 'My father may be many things, but—'

'When did you resign?' Robert demanded in a steely voice.

'It's none of your—'

'By the terms of her contract, Arabella was required to give one month's notice.' Once again it was her father who answered his question. 'But we waived two weeks of it.'

Blue eyes narrowed on Arabella's rebellious expression. 'You left because of the Palfrey book.' It was a statement more than a question this time.

'Incredible, isn't it?' her father said conversationally. 'I always thought Arabella was more like her mother than me, but it appears my daughter inherited my determination.' He shook his head wonderingly. 'I still don't know why Arabella felt so strongly about this book that she felt she had to resign.' He shrugged. 'But nothing I've said to her these past couple of weeks, or indeed Alison…' he smiled lovingly across the room at his bride '…has managed to shake Arabella's decision. It appears my daughter is the only person not pleased with Palfrey's happy ending.'

'Happy ending?' she echoed disgustedly. 'What a strange idea of happiness you men have—and you in the middle of your own wedding, Father! I suppose

Palfrey died in a blaze of glory, and you choose to think of that as a happy ending!' She breathed deeply in her agitation.

'You still haven't read the damned thing, have you?' Robert gave her a frustrated shake, his anger barely contained.

She gave a stubborn shake of her head. 'I told you, I refuse to read about Palfrey's death!'

'Death?' Her father looked stunned. 'But Palfrey doesn't die, Arabella.' He shook his head incredulously. 'He—'

'Martin,' Robert cut in softly, all the time his narrowed gaze fixed on Arabella, 'once again, Arabella and I seem to have chosen an entirely inappropriate place for one of our—verbal displays of passion; would you mind if I took her away from here for a while, so that we might continue this conversation somewhere a little more private? I promise to bring her back later,' he added softly.

'I think that sounds like an excellent idea.' Her father nodded his approval. 'And don't come back— either of you—until this situation is sorted out once and for all.'

Arabella was barely listening to their conversation now, still dazed by the knowledge that Robert hadn't killed Palfrey off after all. Why had no one told her? Why didn't—? Because she had adamantly refused to discuss the book for the last month, had resigned rather than hear anything about it.

But if Robert hadn't killed Palfrey off, what end had he given him...?

'Robert...' her father added softly before the other man could lead her away. 'Might I suggest that this time you do kiss her until she's senseless?'

'I intend doing just that,' Robert assured him grimly.

Arabella gave a startled gasp. But one look at Robert's rigidly held expression and her outraged protest died unspoken in her throat. One word from her now and he was likely to snap completely—and goodness knew what would happen then!

'She has her own apartment now, if you want to go there,' her father confided thoughtfully. 'She moved in yesterday,' he explained, at Robert's questioning look. 'It's a nice place, but probably a bit far away at this moment for what you have in mind.' He winked at the other man. 'And, Arabella—' her father spoke to her gently '—your job will be waiting for you, if—after talking to Robert—you would like to come back.'

'She won't,' Robert told him arrogantly.

Her father quirked questioning brows. 'No?'

'No,' Robert grated determinedly. 'But we'll be back here later,' he promised grimly.

'Take your time,' her father invited lightly.

Robert gave an abrupt nod. 'I intend to.'

Arabella had no chance to protest, either verbally or by physical resistance, as she was firmly and unrelentingly dragged from the hotel.

CHAPTER TEN

'WHERE are we going?' Arabella spoke in a small voice from her seat on the other side of the taxi Robert had put her into minutes ago.

'My hotel,' he answered in a voice that brooked no argument.

Not that she was going to give him one; at the moment she didn't think it would do any good. Robert was so angry that he was rigid, his hands clenched into fists as they rested on his thighs. To argue with him in this particular instance could evoke a response they might both regret. He looked ready to strangle her!

In truth she didn't know what she was arguing about any more. Palfrey hadn't died! She could hardly believe it. She had no idea what ending Robert had chosen for his fictional hero; all she did know—finally—was that he hadn't killed him after all.

Because of what she'd had to say on the subject...? Robert was right—they did need to talk. Although talking didn't seem to be all that he had in mind...

She looked at him from beneath lowered lashes, noting the strength of his jaw, the firmness of his lips, those deep, deep blue eyes. She wanted this man so badly, loved him so much that she didn't care any more about the pain that would follow when he left her life again. She loved him, wanted him to make love to her.

He turned to her within the confines of the taxi,

quirking blond brows. 'Nothing to say?' he prompted dryly.

She met his gaze steadily. 'No.'

He took one of her hands into both of his. 'Arabella, we have a lot of talking to do, but first I just want to make love to you. Is that going to be all right with you?' He frowned.

She smiled at the grimness of his expression. 'Could you try to look a little happier about the prospect?' she teased lightly, a slight catch in her voice. She just wanted to hold him!

He gave a rueful grimace, shaking his head slightly. 'I'm sorry, but there doesn't seem to have been a lot to smile about just recently. Andrew and Stella are sick of the sight of me stamping around, Emma couldn't wait to get away to America, and even the dogs have stayed out of my way the last couple of weeks!'

She hadn't fared much better herself, but she had tried to concentrate her efforts on finding herself another job and somewhere to live, having explained to her father that she welcomed the move. She had succeeded in finding a job and an apartment, had moved the last of her things into the latter only yesterday. She began work as a senior editor with Roach Press on Monday. Her life had changed so much in the last two weeks.

But not her feelings for this man...

'What's been wrong?' She frowned her concern. 'Are you having problems with the new series of books you're writing?'

'Now she acts like my editor!' Robert raised his eyes heavenwards, his hands tightening on hers. 'You are the most complicated woman I have ever met in my life! It's you, woman. *You* are the reason I'm so damned miserable and all of my nearest and dearest just want to stay out of my way!' He grasped her shoulders and shook her slightly in his frustration.

'Me?' She blinked dazedly. 'But—'

'Not here, Arabella,' he ground out fiercely, looking relieved that the taxi had finally arrived at his hotel. 'Let's go upstairs,' he said grimly once they were inside the hotel foyer.

She offered no resistance to this suggestion, too dazed to do anything other than allow herself to be taken upstairs in the lift to his suite. All too soon the two of them were facing each other across the room.

Robert shook his head. 'I know we should talk first, know there are too many things left unsaid, but all I can think of is making love to you.'

She wished he would stop talking about it and just do it!

She frowned up at him as he suddenly gave a triumphant shout of laughter, realising as he swept her up in his arms and carried her into the bedroom that she must have spoken the words out loud. What on earth must he think of her?

What he thought of her was pretty obvious during the next hour; he made love to her as if he were worshipping at a temple, discarding her peach dress so that he could kiss and caress every part of her body, sending Arabella to a sensual delight that she hadn't known existed. But still he didn't take her, even though the throbbing hardness of his own naked body told her how much he wanted to.

'Robert, I want you!' she groaned as she lay beside him on the bed, completely unselfconscious in her nakedness, Robert having left her in no doubt as to how beautiful he found her slender curves.

'I want you too, my darling,' he murmured throatily as his lips sought out the sensitive hollows in her throat.

'Then—'

'My love, you aren't ready yet.' He raised his head to look down at her, his own cheeks flushed with passion.

Not ready? She was going to fall apart in a thousand pieces if she didn't soon know his full possession!

And then he was caressing her again, with his hands, with his lips, and she suddenly knew what he meant: heat pervaded every part of her body, starting in her thighs and slowly, completely burning her.

'Robert?' Her eyes were wide. 'Robert!' she gasped as the pleasure washed over her in uncontrollable waves.

'Now you're ready!' he groaned thankfully, moving above her, gently guiding himself inside her.

The pleasure became so intense, Arabella thought she might faint away completely, clinging to Robert's shoulders as he began to move slowly inside her, building up the passion once again, taking her higher and higher, until they both exploded in a cascade of pleasure that left them gasping.

'It wouldn't have mattered if—I know I don't have the right—God, I'm glad I was the first for you, Arabella!' Robert's arms tightened about her as he cradled her against his side, her head resting on his shoulder, their bodies warm and damp from the heat of their lovemaking.

She laughed happily. 'So am I!' She touched the curling blond hair on his chest.

'Will you marry me?'

She looked up at him sharply, her mouth suddenly dry. He couldn't have just—

'Arabella?' He moved up on one elbow to look down at the shocked expression on her face. 'You don't think I would drag you off from your own father's wedding, take you back to my hotel and make love to you, and not want to marry you?' He frowned darkly. 'What sort of man do you think I am?'

She swallowed hard. Robert wanted to marry her? 'But I'm not beautiful!' she protested—realising even as she said it exactly how ridiculous she must sound. She wasn't beautiful, though, and his wife had been. Very.

Robert looked puzzled, shaking his head slightly. 'How can you say that?' he said slowly. 'Arabella, to me you're the most beautiful woman in the world. How can you doubt that after the way we just made love?'

'You were *married* to the most beautiful woman in the world—'

'Kate!' He fell back against the pillows, his arm flung up over his head, his eyes closed. 'You know about Kate,' he muttered harshly.

Now it was Arabella's turn to move so that she could look down into his face. 'I saw her photograph at the house that time, in Emma's bedroom. I—wasn't prying, Robert. It was just there, and—Robert, please!' She touched his cheek pleadingly, feeling the rigidness of his jaw as she did so. He had asked her to marry him; he couldn't change his mind now!

He opened his eyes. 'Hey, I'm not angry with you.'

His arms came about her, holding her tightly to him. 'If anything I'm angry with myself. I've let that anger rule my life for the last six years. But it's gone now. I would have told you about Kate, Arabella. You would have to know about Emma's mother if you marry me.' He frowned.

'And your wife,' she reminded him gently.

'Yes, she was that too,' he accepted grimly. 'But before we talk about any of this I want you to know I love you. I have since the first day I met you—'

'You can't have done!' Arabella gasped. 'I looked a mess that day. My hair. The glasses. My clothes—'

'Arabella, I love the way you look now, and I'm glad those changes have made you happy, but I loved you the way you were before, too. You had guts getting out of the car that day with the two dogs outside—'

'You had deliberately left them loose to keep A. Atherton at bay!' she accused.

'Guilty,' he accepted dryly. 'But it didn't put you off at all. You came striding up the driveway, the dogs at your heels—'

'And promptly proceeded to make a fool of myself by thinking Andrew was Merlin and you were the gardener!' she remembered with an embarrassed groan.

Robert smiled. 'But you recovered well, determined to discuss the film contract with me, no matter what.'

'And you were just as determined not to do so!'

'For reasons you were made aware of all too soon by the sound of it,' he acknowledged grimly. 'I'll never go back to Hollywood, Arabella. Never allow those people to get their hands on Palfrey. I know them too well, you see, know what they would do to the character. He's my character, Arabella; I have no intention of letting Hollywood suck him in and spit him out so that he's completely unrecognisable.' He frowned darkly. 'They have a way of doing that to people!'

'Kate?' Arabella prompted gently, sensing deep bitterness behind his words, that anger he had spoken of.

'A typical Hollywood brat,' he nodded. 'She's the daughter of one of the studio owners. Beautiful. Talented. And totally immoral.'

'Robert…?' She gasped softly. She had believed he loved his wife, that he had been happy in his marriage…

'Oh, I did love her once, Arabella; never doubt that. We had three good years, but then Emma was conceived, and Kate hated being pregnant, hated everything to do with it, but especially the way it made her look. Her beauty, her perfect figure had always been everything to her, and she felt fat and ugly—'

'Pregnant women aren't fat or ugly,' Arabella protested. 'They're carrying a child, usually evidence of a shared love.'

Robert's arms tightened about her as he buried his face in her neck. 'I knew you would feel like that. I just knew it.'

She was sure most women felt the same way. But perhaps not one to whom the way she looked was everything… Arabella had been running away from this man ever since she'd realised she was in love with him, and who his wife had been. Now she found it wasn't as she had thought at all. Perhaps she needn't have run after all. She had always wondered why it was that Robert had custody of Emma…

Robert moved back slightly, shaking his head. 'Kate hated it. As for the birth—she took one look at Emma afterwards and then gave her into the care of the nanny she had hired before the baby was born. As far as I'm aware she didn't even look at her again until she was three years old—young enough to be cute to look at and shown off, but old enough to do what she was told.

'As for me...' He sighed raggedly. 'I couldn't bear to touch Kate after she rejected our daughter.' His expression was grim as he remembered that time. 'As a punishment for that she took a string of lovers. She married the latest one in a blaze of Hollywood hype after our divorce.'

'I never realised...' Arabella groaned, absolutely stunned at this breaking of a Hollywood myth. No wonder Robert hated Hollywood and everything to do with it!

'Neither did anyone else,' he acknowledged harshly. 'Because until the kidnapping Kate was perfectly happy with the arrangement. She could live exactly the way she wanted but also within the respectability of marriage. And she held the trump card. All of my requests for a divorce ended in her telling me she would claim custody of Emma...!'

'Oh, God...' Arabella knew only too well how much he loved his daughter. And how much Emma loved him in return.

'Exactly,' he said bleakly. 'That was something I could never allow. So I stayed with her, buried myself in my own work, turned a blind eye to Kate's behaviour. As long as she left Emma and me alone, I didn't care any more. But the kidnapping, the fact that it was her father who came up with the money, allowed her to opt out of the marriage and still carry on looking like Snow White.

'I was cast as the baddie,' he recalled bitterly. 'But I was willing to accept that, if I could at last be free of that loveless marriage. The one thing I asked in return for allowing myself to be cast in that role was that I have complete custody of Emma.' His mouth twisted. 'As Kate had never really wanted her in the first place, that suited her all too well!'

It all sounded dreadful. Arabella couldn't even begin to imagine what it must have been like to live like that. If only she had known about his sham of a marriage before. The ghost she had been running away from wasn't one that could hurt her. Robert loved her.

'Emma's in the States with Kate at the moment,' Robert told her ruefully. 'Up until now I've tried to protect her from the influences of Hollywood and her mother's life over there, but falling in love with you has shown me that I can't go on hiding Emma away for ever. One day she will have to make up her own mind about her mother.

'Kate is still married to the same man, has no other children, claims she's happy at last, that she loves Emma and wants to get to know her daughter. In the past I've always refused Kate's requests for Emma to visit her in America.' He shrugged. 'Only ever agreed to her seeing her occasionally for a few hours in London. The last time was the morning before the three of *us* ended up having lunch at Mario's,' he added pointedly.

That was the reason why Emma had looked surprised when Arabella had asked her how she had enjoyed her shopping trip!

'I took Emma over to Kate in the States earlier this

week, made sure she was settled, that the two of them seemed to be getting on, before coming back so that I could be here for you at your father's wedding,' Robert explained gently. 'I didn't want you to have to go through that alone.'

'But I'm happy for them,' she protested. 'Really I am.'

'You looked upset that day in the restaurant when you saw them together.' He frowned. 'Even more so later on when your father told me about the wedding. And you've moved into your own apartment,' he reminded her.

'I was upset that day in the restaurant because you obviously found Alison very attractive,' Arabella admitted uncomfortably. 'You seemed to admire my father's choice of bride when he told you about the wedding. As for my apartment, I've moved because I wanted to, because—'

'You've been jealous of Alison because of me?' Robert cut in incredulously.

'Yes,' she sighed. 'I—'

'Arabella, you love me too!' he announced triumphantly.

'Well, of course I do,' she confirmed impatiently. 'Why else would I be here with you?'

'Arabella, I told you at least fifteen minutes ago that I'm in love with you, and so far you haven't reciprocated,' he reproved her indulgently.

They were naked in each other's arms, had just made love so beautifully she could have cried; of course she loved him. But he was right; she hadn't actually said as much...

'I loved the part of you I knew through your books

even before I met you,' she admitted shyly. 'Robert, you are Palfrey.'

'And you love him too, don't you?' He nodded slowly. 'I realised that the first day. You were absolutely devastated when Emma said he was to die,' he recalled softly. 'It was your reaction that made me sit down and rethink my decision. If you felt that way, felt prepared to try to save Palfrey, then other people were going to feel the same way. I realised then that, although I may have the power of life and death over Palfrey, I could also hurt people very badly by wielding that power.'

'And Palfrey's end?' she asked breathlessly, so glad she was the main reason he had changed his mind.

'It isn't really an end, Arabella, but a beginning! Palfrey falls in love, gets married, and lives happily ever after. And his author would like to meet the same fate. With you.' He cupped her chin so that she was looking directly up into his face, held mesmerised by those deep blue eyes. 'Your answer, Arabella; will you marry me?'

She could marry this man, spend the rest of her life with him. They could even have children of their own. She might even have already conceived. 'Oh, yes, Robert.' She threw her arms up about his neck. 'I'll marry you. I'll marry you! I want to spend the rest of my life making you happy.'

He bent to kiss her tenderly on the lips. 'You are the most incredible woman I've ever met in my life,' he told her admiringly. 'I still can't believe you actually resigned because of Palfrey.' He shook his head indulgently.

'He's real to me, Robert. So real. Because he's you, can't you see? Once I had met you, come to know the person behind Palfrey, to let him die would have been like letting you die.' Her arms tightened about him. 'I couldn't bear that, Robert. I love you so very much, you see,' she admitted huskily.

'I tried so hard to get you to read that last Palfrey book,' he groaned. 'Wanted you to see what effect your words had had on me. But you were so damned stubborn—'

'And you weren't stubborn, I suppose, when you could have just told me that you had changed your mind? Besides, you can't be angry with me,' she added teasingly. 'Not when you've said I'm the most incredible woman you've ever met in your life!'

'Oh, you're that too,' he nodded, smiling. 'Arabella, at this moment I want you again so very badly. But we have a lifetime to make love, to tell each other how we feel, and I did promise your father we would return to the wedding—'

'My father, and his wedding, can just wait!' She moved so that Robert was the one to be lying on his back on the bed, with Arabella draped over him. 'I'm not completely senseless yet,' she added provocatively as she lowered her head towards his.

Robert gave a triumphant laugh as he swept her into his arms. 'A demanding wife; I think I'm going to like that very much indeed!'

Wife. Robert's wife. *She* was going to like that very much indeed. For the rest of her life.

EVER HAD ONE OF THOSE DAYS?

TO DO:

- ☑ late for a super-important meeting, you discover the cat has eaten your panty hose

- ☑ while you work through lunch, the rest of the gang goes out and finds a one-hour, once-in-a-lifetime 90% off sale at the most exclusive store in town (Oh, and they also get to meet Brad Pitt who's filming a movie across the street.)

- ☑ you discover that your intimate phone call with your boyfriend was on company-wide intercom

- ☑ finally at the end of a long and exasperating day, you escape from it all with an entertaining, humorous and always romantic Love & Laughter book!

ENJOY
LOVE & LAUGHTER™
EVERY DAY!

For a preview, turn the page....

"DARLING, YOU SOUND like a broken cappuccino machine," murmured Charlotte, her voice oozing disapproval.

Russell juggled the receiver while attempting to sit up in bed, but couldn't. If he *sounded* like a wreck over the phone, he could only imagine what he looked like.

"What mischief did you and your friends get into at your bachelor's party last night?" she continued.

She always had a way of saying "your friends" as though they were a pack of degenerate water buffalo. Professors deserved to be several notches higher up on the food chain, he thought. Which he would have said if his tongue wasn't swollen to twice its size.

"You didn't do anything...bad...did you, Russell?"

"Bad." His laugh came out like a bark.

"Bad as in *naughty*."

He heard her piqued tone but knew she'd never admit to such a base emotion as jealousy. Charlotte Maday, the woman he was to wed in a week, came from a family who bled blue. Exhibiting raw emotion was akin to burping in public.

After agreeing to be at her parents' pool party by noon, he untangled himself from the bed sheets and stumbled to the bathroom.

"Pool party," he reminded himself. He'd put on his best front and accommodate Char's request. Make the family rounds, exchange a few pleasantries, play the role she liked best: the erudite, cultured English literature professor. After fulfilling his duties, he'd slink into some lawn chair, preferably one in the shade, and nurse his hangover.

He tossed back a few aspirin and splashed cold water on his face. Grappling for a towel, he squinted into the mirror.

Then he jerked upright and stared at his reflection, blinking back drops of water. "Good Lord. They stuck me in a wind tunnel."

His hair, usually neatly parted and combed, sprang from his head as though he'd been struck by lightning. "Can too many Wild Turkeys do that?" he asked himself as he stared with horror at his reflection.

Something caught his eye in the mirror. Russell's gaze dropped.

"What in the—"

Over his pectoral muscle was a small patch of white. A bandage. Gingerly, he pulled it off.

Underneath, on his skin, was not a wound but a small, neat drawing.

"A red heart?" His voice cracked on the word *heart*. Something—a word?—was scrawled across it.

"Good Lord," he croaked. "I got a tattoo. A heart tattoo with the name Liz on it."

Not Charlotte. Liz!

Harlequin Women Know Romance When They See It.

And they'll see it on **ROMANCE CLASSICS**, the new 24-hour TV channel devoted to romantic movies and original programs like the special **Harlequin** Showcase of Authors & Stories.

The **Harlequin** Showcase of Authors & Stories introduces you to many of your favorite romance authors in a program developed exclusively for Harlequin readers.

Watch for the **Harlequin** Showcase of Authors & Stories series beginning in the summer of 1997.

ROMANCE CLASSICS

If you're not receiving ROMANCE CLASSICS, call your local cable operator or satellite provider and ask for it today!

Escape to the network of your dreams.

Take 4 bestselling love stories FREE

Plus get a FREE surprise gift!

Special Limited-time Offer

Mail to Harlequin Reader Service®

P.O. Box 609
Fort Erie, Ontario
L2A 5X3

YES! Please send me 4 free Harlequin Presents® novels and my free surprise gift. Then send me 6 brand-new novels every month, which I will receive months before they appear in bookstores. Bill me at the low price of $3.24 each—plus 25¢ delivery and GST *. That's the complete price and a savings of over 10% off the cover prices—quite a bargain! I understand that accepting the books and gift places me under no obligation ever to buy any books. I can always return a shipment and cancel at any time. Even if I never buy another book from Harlequin, the 4 free books and the surprise gift are mine to keep forever.

306 BPA A3UD

Name _____ (PLEASE PRINT)

Address _____ Apt. No. _____

City _____ Province _____ Postal Code _____

This offer is limited to one order per household and not valid to present Harlequin Presents® subscribers. *Terms and prices are subject to change without notice. Canadian residents will be charged applicable provincial taxes and GST.

CPRES-696   ©1990 Harlequin Enterprises Limited

Free Gift Offer

With a Free Gift proof-of-purchase
from any Harlequin® book, you can receive
a beautiful cubic zirconia pendant.

This stunning marquise-shaped stone is a genuine cubic
zirconia—accented by an 18" gold tone necklace.
(Approximate retail value $19.95)

Send for yours today...
compliments of ◈HARLEQUIN®

To receive your free gift, a cubic zirconia pendant, send us one original proof-of-purchase, photocopies not accepted, from the back of any Harlequin Romance®, Harlequin Presents®, Harlequin Temptation®, Harlequin Superromance®, Harlequin Intrigue®, Harlequin American Romance®, or Harlequin Historicals® title available at your favorite retail outlet, together with the Free Gift Certificate, plus a check or money order for $1.65 U.S./$2.15 CAN. (do not send cash) to cover postage and handling, payable to Harlequin Free Gift Offer. We will send you the specified gift. Allow 6 to 8 weeks for delivery. Offer good until December 31, 1997, or while quantities last. Offer valid in the U.S. and Canada only.

Free Gift Certificate

Name: _____

Address: _____

City: _____ State/Province: _____ Zip/Postal Code: _____

Mail this certificate, one proof-of-purchase and a check or money order for postage and handling to: HARLEQUIN FREE GIFT OFFER 1997. In the U.S.: 3010 Walden Avenue, P.O. Box 9071, Buffalo NY 14269-9057. In Canada: P.O. Box 604, Fort Erie, Ontario L2Z 5X3.

FREE GIFT OFFER   084-KEZ
ONE PROOF-OF-PURCHASE
To collect your fabulous FREE GIFT, a cubic zirconia pendant, you must include this original proof-of-purchase for each gift with the properly completed Free Gift Certificate.

084-KEZR